I0650517

Edmund Evans, Maria Elizabeth Budden, Robert S. Bross, John
William Orr

Always Happy

Anecdotes of Felix and His Sister Serena

Edmund Evans, Maria Elizabeth Budden, Robert S. Bross, John William Orr

Always Happy

Anecdotes of Felix and His Sister Serena

ISBN/EAN: 9783337139247

Printed in Europe, USA, Canada, Australia, Japan

Cover: Foto ©Andreas Hilbeck / pixelio.de

More available books at **www.hansebooks.com**

ALWAYS HAPPY.

Illustrated.

New York:
Published by James Miller,
(SUCCESSOR TO C. S. FRANCIS & CO.)
522 Broadway.

ALWAYS HAPPY;

OR

Anecdotes

OF

FELIX AND HIS SISTER SERENA.

NEW YORK:

PUBLISHED BY JAMES MILLER,

(SUCCESSOR TO C. S. FRANCIS & CO.,)

522 BROADWAY.

MDCCCLXIII.

DEDICATION.

In the winter of 1812-13, a little circle of young children were accustomed to be amused by short tales, made at the moment, for their amusement and instruction.—The beneficial effects which these little Stories produced in the conduct of the young listeners, first gave the idea of writing the following Tale; thus hoping to impress a more permanent advantage. In this hope an anxious Mother dedicates this little Work to her six beloved children.

DEVONSHIRE.

CONTENTS.

CHAPTER I.

CHAPTER II.

CHAPTER III.

CHAPTER IV.

1*

CHAPTER V.

CHAPTER VI.

CHAPTER VII.

CHAPTER VIII.

CHAPTER IX.

CHAPTER X.

ALWAYS HAPPY.

CHAPTER I.

INTRODUCTION.—A Cure for Discontent.—The Mischiefs
of Silly Fears.—Courage always amiable.

IN the neighborhood of a small country town
lived Felix and his sister Serena. They loved
each other tenderly, and were happy in having
kind parents, who were always attentive to
their improvement and happiness. The father
of Felix was not rich, but he was contented with what he had. His name was not
graced with any title of nobility: he was
neither a lord nor a duke. He was simply an
honest man; a title self-earned, and placing
its possessor amongst all good men. He was

compassionate, he was pious, and all his neighbors loved and respected him.

Felix had many good qualities, but he had also many faults; he was sometimes passionate, sometimes idle, sometimes self-conceited. Of these faults he knew he could cure himself, for his father had told him so: and, though he was not remarkably clever, he had sense enough to resolve to conquer his faults. In the end, as might be expected, he succeeded: and you will hear how, by his constant endeavors, he grew up to be almost as good a man as his father.

Serena was younger than her brother; she was not a pretty little girl, but she looked so clean, so good-humoured, and so cheerful, that she was loved by all who knew her; nobody ever thought whether she was handsome or not. Yet Serena, like her brother, sometimes did wrong. She was apt to cry about trifles, was very careless and forgetful, and, in short.

like most little children, had many faults to be corrected. Yet, by minding all her mother said to her, and every day trying to improve by little and little, I assure you, she became a very amiable, sensible woman.

Though faults can be certainly, they cannot be easily, cured. Those who have the greatest faults to amend, must of course have the most merit when they do conquer them. When Felix, in the midst of a sulky fit, reasoned himself into a good temper, and, instead of sullen looks, turned to his sister with a good-humoured smile, his heart always told him how properly he was behaving. And when Serena, in the midst of her tears, recollected for what a silly trifle she cried, the moment she wiped her eyes and became cheerful, she felt a kind pleasure, which all must feel when they heartily try to do what is right.

Now the methods by which this little boy

2

and this little girl learned to improve in
knowledge and in virtue, and the happy life
they led, will, I think, make a very pretty
story, and amuse us all, I dare say, very much.

It was Winter; the snow lay thick on the
ground, the frost had hardened the water, and
the cold was very severe.

"Oh! how cold it is, how very cold!"
said Serena, and her little face seemed drawing
up into a cry. "True, my love," said her
mother, "we are all cold, and we must bear it
patiently." Serena looked as if she would
not bear it patiently: her mother went on—
"Think, my Serena, how many poor little
children have other evils, as great as the frost,
to bear, and those in addition to it. Without
clothes, without food, without fire, think what
they must suffer."—"But, mamma, to think
they are worse does not make me better."—
"It ought to make you more patient, since
you have so much less to suffer; it ought to

make you thankful, since you have so much
more to enjoy. Look at this warm frock, this
blazing fire, this bowl of smoking bread and
milk! are not these comforts, Serena?"—
"Oh! yes, mamma, great comfort," smacking
her lips, as she tasted her nice breakfast.
"And are you particularly good, that you
should possess such advantages above hundreds
of little starving girls?" Serena blushed, and
put down her spoon. "I fear not, mamma."
—"Well, then, my love, try to thank a good
God who has been so bountiful to you, by
gratefully and cheerfully enjoying the many
blessings He has showered upon you; and,
since your own lot can produce only smiles,
let the next tear I see twinkling in your eye
come there for the real sorrows of another, not
for the fancied woes of yourself." As her
mother said this, she kissed her little Serena,
and the happy child felt in her heart that she
had indeed a great deal to be thankful for.

Felix now entered the room wi.h a glowing face, and, running up to his mother, "Oh! mother," said he, "here is a poor, shivering, old man at the door—may I give him something? You know, I was the best child yesterday." "Well, then, take your reward; here are some halfpence, go, give them to the poor, shivering, old man." Felix joyfully executed the commission, and, when he returned, told his sister that the old man had said "God bless you, my dear!"—"I hope," answered Serena, "that I shall behave the best to-day, and then to-morrow somebody shall say so to me."—"What is all this?" said their father. "I thought, my dear," turning to his wife, "I thought you never relieved common street-beggars, such as this man was."—"Nor do I," replied his wife, "at any other season of the year; but at Christmas, I find, it is a general practice for every housekeeper to contribute his mite, by

Felix and his Sister Serena.

which means a useful sum is collected; I therefore add my little offering to the store."—" And whichever of the children behaves best you make your almoner?"—"I do."—"Then, my love, be assured you make the best possible use of your mite." The breakfast was now over. The children flew eagerly to their books; reading, writing, and spelling, each came forward in turn. Felix and his father devoted half an hour to Latin grammar, whilst Serena, bringing her stool, sat down to work by her mother; she was hemming a handkerchief for her brother, and as her fingers swiftly passed over her work, her little tongue was equally busy.—"Pray. mamma, when shall I learn music?"—"I do not think. Serena, you will ever learn it."—"Never learn music! Why. mamma, I thought every body learned it; you know you have."—"Yes, my dear, because I had a good deal of leisure."—"And so have I, I am sure."—

2*

" And yet, Serena, though you have so much time, I do not find that your brother's handkerchief is finished yet."—" But that is such tedious work, the same thing over and over again."—" And do you think you could learn music without going over and over again? Nothing, you know, requires more perseverance than learning to play on a pianoforte. Did not Miss Wood tell us she had practised six hours a day for many years?"—" Yes, mamma."—" And what else did she say?" —" I remember, for it surprised me very much; she said that now she did not open her instrument once in a month."—" But yet she had time?"—" Oh! yes, because she said she made all her father's shirts, which he would have had made out of the house, but she preferred doing them."—" Then, I suppose, having tried both, she found needlework one of the most amusing as well as the most useful employments."—" Then, shall I never learn anything but needlework?"—"I hope you will: but you must learn that well first. for it is necessary. Music, drawing, and dancing are unnecessary, and must therefore be only thought of as amusements: as such, should your taste dispose you to any of these acquirements, I shall very willingly allow you to follow them."—"But French I shall certainly learn?"—"Yes, French is now almost become a necessary part of education, and I hope you will not only read it, but speak it."—"I am sure I shall never have courage to speak it."—"Do not be sure, Serena; suppose yourself in company with a Frenchwoman, who could not speak one word of English; would not you be happy to relieve her distress, and address her in her own language?"—"Yes, if I had resolution."—"You must never want resolution to do what is right. As soon as you have determined what is most proper for you to do, you must steadily perform it, whatever exertion it may cost you. I would not have my Serena thought bold or forward, but I hope I shall always see her possess a modest confidence. However, your work is finished ; we will therefore talk more of this another time ; now bring your bonnet and coat, and we will take our morning's walk."—"In the snow ?"— " On the roads the snow is trodden down, and we shall find a good path."

The walk did not prove so unpleasant as Serena expected, and she returned home with an excellent appetite for her dinner. The day closed in early, and the family drew round their cheerful fire. "And now, papa," said Felix, " do tell us a story ; you know we dearly love stories, and this is just the time to enjoy them." His father smiled—" Will you, then, promise to be quiet ? I do not like talking in a noise."—" Indeed I will be very still," cried Felix. " And I too," exclaimed

Serena, "I will be as still as a mouse!"—
"A mouse is not always still, Serena: and I
can tell you a tale where a mouse frightened
two little girls most terribly."—"A mouse
frighten girls! Nay, now, papa, you are
only joking." "No, I assure you I read it in
a clever book, and I dare say it was true."—
"Pray, then, dear papa, let us hear how a
mouse could be so terrible."—"You are
mistaken, Serena; the mouse was a very
pretty mouse, and, except in nibbling bread
and cheese, perfectly harmless; it was only
the girls that were silly; but you shall hear.
One fine moonlight night, two tired girls went
to bed; they had been spending the day with
a kind aunt, who had given them a nice plum-
cake. Now this cake was too large to be
eaten at once; it was therefore deposited in a
box that stood on a table in their chamber.
The lid of the box had been broken; it could
not therefore be properly shut. The little

girls, tenderly locked in each other's arms, soon fell sweetly asleep. Silence reigned around, and their slumbers remained long unbroken: at length a poor little half-starved mouse crept from her hiding-place in the wainscot, and began peeping about in the hope of finding something to satisfy her appetite. It was not long before the smell of the rich cake directed her to the box on the table; she carefully crept into it, and with rapture devoured its contents. A slight noise in the adjoining room, and the distant mewing of a cat, alarmed the timid plunderer; she attempted to spring from the box, but in her fright she drew it to the edge of the table, whence it fell to the floor, with a loud crash, and, turning over in the fall, secured the poor mouse beneath it. The unusual noise awakened the sisters. 'Bless me!' cried one, almost breathless with fear and surprise, 'Bless me! Ann, what can that noise be?'—'It was very

terrible indeed,' replied Ann; 'I cannot
account for it, but I dare say it will do us no
harm.'—'No harm? Oh! it must do us
harm.'—'Why, Mary, I never heard of a noise
hurting any body,' said Ann, laughing at her
sister.—'But it may be robbers, dear Ann;
what shall we do?'—'Be quiet, certainly; if
it be robbers, we shall hear more; they cannot
long keep still.'—'Dear me, how you talk!
and I am so frightened!'—'But pray do not
be frightened; for, depend upon it, thieves do
not break into houses to steal little girls,'—
'Indeed, indeed, I cannot lie still.'—'But,
dear Mary, what shall we do?'—'I don't
know; you are the eldest, you must advise
me.'—'I advise you to go to sleep. For why
should we disturb the servants, who are all
comfortably asleep? And, indeed there is
nothing to fear.' As she said this, the kind
and sensible Ann drew aside the curtain; and,
the moon shining clear into the room, they

quickly perceived the box overthrown. At
this they both laughed; and, in forming
various conjectures how it could possibly have
fallen from the table, they again fell asleep.
Early the next morning, their mother, as
usual, entered their chamber, and was immediately informed of their last night's wonderful
adventure. She was much amused by the
conjectures each had formed respecting this
magical overthrow, and very frankly declared
she thought it had been occasioned by a
mouse. 'No, indeed, mother,' said Mary,
'you must be wrong; a mouse could not
possibly move this great box.'—'I do not say
a mouse could move this box to any distance,
but I think, by its endeavors to get to the cake,
it might so shake it as to draw it to the edge
of the table. and then you know a slight touch
would cause it to fall.'—'Oh! but the noise
we heard was so great! It was greater than
a hundred mice could make. I am sure it

could not be a mouse.'—'You are very
positive, little girl, said her mother; 'however,
we will take up the box, and the scattered
cake.' She did so, and instantly the poor
imprisoned mouse rushed across the room, and
darted into her hole. Mary screamed. 'My
dear child, why that scream? will it preserve
you from danger? Or is it only to show how
very silly you can be?' Mary blushed. 'Do
you think yourself or the poor little animal
which has just escaped from us, has most cause
for fear? You, whose single hand could not
only seize the body, but crush the life, of the
unprotected, feeble mouse. Fie, Mary! you
make me ashamed of you. But perhaps you
would wish to be pitied for your delicate
weakness?'—'No indeed, mother.'—'I say
no indeed, too, Mary: and beg of you to try
rather to be respected for your resolution, than
despised, as you surely must be, for such
contemptible fears.'"

3

"Papa, that is indeed a droll story," said Serena. "I am thinking," cried Felix, "if this had happened on a dark night without the moon to show the box on the floor, what Mary would have done."—"I suppose she would have alarmed all the family," said his mother. "Yes," added his father, "and then, after all the confusion, behold the poor mouse discovered as the cause of her unfounded fears!"—"How they would all have laughed at her!" exclaimed Serena: "yet, mamma, I have seen grown-up ladies frightened at less things than a mouse. I remember a spider frightened Mrs.——."—"Hush! my love, never remember the silly or improper actions of your friends. Spiders certainly are a very insufficient cause for fear; and since we think so, let us endeavor to conquer all such weaknesses. By the exertion of a little sense, this may easily be done, particularly by young people. And one of the best means of con-

quering fear is instantly to investigate its cause.
A friend of mine, going at night into her
chamber, by chance extinguished her candle;
in attempting to grope her way to the door,
she was startled by something that appeared,
though very indistinctly, like a white figure
standing near the window. She paused for a
moment; but, instantly recollecting herself,
walked boldly up to the object; and what do
you think it was? Nothing more nor less than
her own long white dressing-gown, which she
herself had hung there, and on which the dim
light from the window shone."—"That was
laughable indeed."—" Yes; and I myself had
also an equally curious adventure. Your dear
grandmother was often an invalid. In one of
her illnesses, I was her nurse, and often,
during the night, had occasion to go into
different parts of the house. One night,
something was required from the closet of our
common sitting-room. I descended slowly

down the creaking stairs, and, entering the room, soon found what I wanted. Hastily returning, I was a good deal surprised by observing a strong light play on the opposite wall, after my candle was removed into the passage. This I could not account for, as the fire was out, and myself the only person moving about the house."—"Dear mamma, what are you going to tell us?" "I put down my light on the stairs, and resolved on discovering whence this phenomenon, and boldly returned into the room. The miraculous light still beamed. What could it be? That was soon explained, for, turning round, I found that the light from my candle, entering through the half-opened door, gleamed on a large mirror, which reflected the rays to the opposite wall. This was a plain and simple effect. I was satisfied, and quickly returned to my expecting invalid."—"Have you no more such charming stories?"—"I do not remember any more just now; besides, your supper-hour is arrived."—"Oh! but we do not want our supper now; we would rather have more stories."—"Every thing in its proper place; we must never jostle out one business for another; we must now attend to our evening occupations. Yet let me, before we quit the subject, entreat you to bear these little stories in your mind; and never, by want of resolution, hoard up for yourselves the misery of groundless fears. Be assured, courage is equally amiable in woman as in man: and that the moment we begin to pity the fancifully timid, we also begin to despise. Fear nothing but to do wrong."

CHAPTER II.

A Remedy for Peevishness.—Active Assistance better than
useless Sympathy.—Fine Clothes often troublesome.—
Wishing very foolish.

IN a few days the snow had disappeared; yet
a keen frost continued to bind the earth.
The sun shone cheerfully, and Felix, after his
morning's avocations, had been enjoying, with
his sister, the beauty of the weather. Tired
at length with play, he stood watching some
laborers at work in an adjoining field, till the
cold seized on his hands and fingers. Shivering and cross, he returned to the parlor,
where his mother sat at work. The fire soon
relieved his chilled fingers, but a discontented
gloom hung on his countenance. The watch
pointed at twelve. Felix wanted his dinner,
and was angry that the time did not pass

quicker. His sister, in endeavoring to reach
the fire, very slightly touched his elbow ; this
he called beating him : and he was altogether
so peevish, that at last his mother asked him
what was the matter. Felix did not answer,
for he really did not know what was the
matter with himself. "Are you cold, my
dear ?"—"No, mother."—"Are you hungry ?"—"No, mother."—"Yet you wish for
your dinner ?"—"Yes, because that will pass
away the time a little."—"Pass away the
time, Felix ! 'the precious time !' for every
moment of which we are to be accountable to
God. Surely, my dear boy, you do not think
of what you say! Can time be recalled, that
thus you would throw it away ? It was only
yesterday you wished the morning had been an
hour longer, and to-day you are going to throw
an hour away." "Ah! but yesterday I was
happy." "And are you unhappy to-day,
Felix ?" "No, not quite unhappy, but very

uncomfortable."—" Are you sick ? "—" No,
mother."—" Are you in pain ? "—" No, mother."—" Neither sick nor in pain, neither
hungry nor cold, and yet very uncomfortable !
Ah ! Felix, I see what is the matter with you,
—you are discontented ; and, by giving way
to your ill-humor, you are making both your
sister and me suffer from it." Felix looked
down. " Now, as it is always my wish to
remove all your complaints and teach you, by
being good, to be always happy, I will shew
you what I think will prevent you ever again
being discontented. Go and ask the cook for
that mug of gruel I bade her make: you,
Serena, shall carry this parcel of soft linen,
and we will visit the poor woman who lies
sick in the village." The gruel was brought ;
and Felix, carrying it, walked silently beside
his mother. They soon reached the cottage:
on entering it, they were met by an old
woman, who, in spite of age and infirmity,

Here, on a low bed without curtains, lay the suffering
invalid.

was busily occupied in washing; a young girl,
ten years old, the eldest of six children, was
cleaning potatoes for their homely dinner.
The other children were playing in different
parts of the room. The father was absent,
having left his cobbler's stall to fetch some
medicines for his wife. Felix followed his
mother up a broken staircase, which opened
into the only chamber the cottage afforded.
Here, on a low bed without curtains, lay the
suffering invalid. By over exertions for her
young family, she had by some means sprained
her arm, which, from mismanagement, had
gathered to a sore. The wound had become
exquisitely painful; and, though she uttered no
complaint, the large drops that trickled down
her pale face proved how great was her
suffering.

Serena was affected to tears. Her mother
kindly addressed the poor woman: "I fear
you are in great pain." "Yes, madam.

indeed I am."—" But you do not complain."
—" No, surely, madam, that would do no
good, but only distress my family." Felix
looked at his mother, whilst his heart severely
smote him. The woman continued, " Alas!
madam, my greatest pain is to be such a
trouble to all around me ; such an expense
to my husband."—" Be comforted, good
woman ; your patience deserves our best
assistance : and, be assured, you shall have
it."—" God bless you, madam! God reward
you for what you have already done for me ! "
The scene was now beginning to be too
affecting ; Serena's tears were accompanied
by half-suppressed sobs ; her mother took her
hand, and, promising to call again, hastily left
the cottage.

As they walked home, she asked Felix
what he thought of the scene he had just
witnessed. " Think! Oh! mother, I *feel* I
should never be discontented again." " Let

the resolution sink into your heart, my child, and teach you not only to pity the sorrows of your fellow-creatures, but also to remember the many blessings by which you are surrounded. You see that, even in the greatest bodily anguish, patience can lessen the suffering; but when enjoying, as you now do, health, youth, and vigor, it is wicked to have your brow clouded by glooms." "Indeed, mother, I do think I never shall be gloomy again."

"I hope not; it is our duty to be cheerful; it is our duty to enjoy the good bestowed on us: and if you try, depend upon it you will find something or other that can always cheer and enliven you. But, my gentle Serena, pray wipe away these tears. I do not blame you for having felt so much; sympathy is due to distress; but shall I tell you what is even better than weeping over the miseries of another?"—"What, mamma?"—"Endeavoring to relieve them."—"Ah, if I could do that!"—"Dry your eyes, then, and think if there is not anything you can do. Whilst you continue to cry, you may hurt yourself, but you cannot benefit the object of your commiseration."—"There, now I have wiped my eyes: now tell me what such a poor little weak child as I can do."—"You are little, certainly, and not very strong; yet I believe you have as much use of your fingers as I have."—"Mamma, I know what you mean, —work for her."—"Yes, my love; did you not observe how much her bed-gown was tattered, and her cap worn out?"—"Oh! yes, yes, dear mamma; let us go directly home, and set to work."—"Though I am not fond of doing things in a hurry, yet in so good a cause we will set aside common rules, and make all the haste in our power."—"I can do nothing," said Felix, sorrowfully. "Indeed, brother, you can; if papa will let you, I mean."—"What, Serena?"—"Why, have

Serena and her Mother visiting the poor family.

you not a shilling in your box?" "To be sure I have; how glad I am it is not spent! And see! papa is coming to meet us. I will directly ask his leave to give my shilling to the poor woman." His father not only assented to his request, but added another shilling to the store. The evening was happily spent: Serena worked very fast and very well; a new cap and bed-gown were completed by her and her mother. The next morning the party again visited the cottage. With a beating heart, Felix made his little offering: with sparkling eyes, Serena produced her handywork. As she assisted the woman in putting on the bed-gown, her mother, in a whisper, asked if this was not better than only giving her useless tears to the poor sufferer. "Better, indeed, mamma; ah! how much better!"—"Learn, then, my dear little girl, to check, rather than encourage, that sensibility which renders us useless to those for whom we feel; and engrave it on your heart, that one active exertion of our power, however small or humble, is worth a whole age of indolent unassisting pity."

They now returned home, and Felix hastened to find his father, and inform him of all that had passed. His father was in the parlor, chatting with some visiters. Felix knew that this was not the time to speak; he therefore waited patiently till he should be alone. He heard, however, with surprise, that his father, in a mild but firm manner, declined subscribing to some charity which was spoken of, and which was to be advertised in the newspapers. As soon as the guests withdrew, "Do tell me, my dear father, why you did not subscribe to that charity just now."—"I could not afford it."—"And yet you have always money for our poor neighbors; and last week, you know, you gave soup to every cottager."—"Very true,

Felix; that certainly cost money: and because I have done that, I cannot give money now. I am not able to subscribe to both public and private charity; I prefer the latter, because I have the objects immediately under my observation. I wish I could do both; those are happy who can: but I will never draw from the hoard sacred to my obscure neighbor, to place my name in a public print, and leave the helpless villager unnoticed, that I may ostentatiously blazon my charity to the world. Do you understand me, Felix?"—"Perfectly, papa: you approve of charity in any form, and for any motive; but you think private charity the most beneficial."—"Exactly so; and now tell me the history of your morning's adventure." Felix very feelingly described what he had seen; and, being soon joined by his mother and sister, they all continued talking some time on the subject. Serena lamented she had nothing to bestow. " You have given your time, my dear; and what other gift could be equally valuable from you, or equally useful to them?" replied her mother. "But, mamma, shall I never have money to give?"—"I hope you will; as soon as you are old enough, your papa and I intend to allow you a certain sum for your clothes and other expenses." "I shall be glad of that; because then I can be very, very careful, and save something for the poor, and do as you often have done, mamma, —go without a new cap, or a new ribbon, and give the money they would have cost to the sick and needy. How much I shall like that!"—"I am glad, my little girl, that your wish for riches is so connected with the intentions of benevolence. I hope it will always be so. As long as you dress neatly and clean, and do not require me to make up the deficiencies of your wardrobe, I shall think you quite at liberty to give away what you

please."—"Oh! mamma, I will take care
never to want things that are necessary to
make me neat; for, if you were to have to
buy shoes for me, it would be your money,
and not mine, you know, that was bestowed
in charity."—"I see you understand the rights
of property, Serena," said her father, smiling.
"As it is now my turn to speak, I will tell
you something that will, I am sure, give you
pleasure. You are going to spend to-morrow
at your grandpapa's: you will meet your
cousins there, and, I hope, spend a very
happy day together."

"We shall be sure to be happy, for grand
papa is so kind: and we shall have plenty of
play, for my cousins love play dearly," said
Felix. "Yes," said Serena, "and they are
always smart, so smart! Pray, mamma, what
dress shall I wear to-morrow?"—"The same
as usual, Serena—a clean white frock." "And
no sash, mamma: no pretty blue shoes, like
4*

my cousins'?"—"No, my dear: a sash is perfectly useless; and as for blue shoes, they are too expensive." Serena sighed. "Will your grandpapa love you less in plain clothes?" —"No, mother," exclaimed Felix, "I am sure he won't; for we all think Serena is his favorite."—"What can that be for, I wonder!"—"I suppose, because she is the best tempered." Serena smiled. "Or, do you think, my love, you will be more comfortable in blue than black shoes?" Serena looked at her brother. Felix laughed, and said, "I understand your looks, Serena. Do you know, mother, that, at our very last visit, my cousins could not go with us to see a beautiful new peacock grandpapa kept in the yard, because they were afraid of dirtying their pretty blue shoes; and cousin Fanny cried for an hour because she had stained her sash with preserves."—"So much for the joys of a smart dress; besides which, let me remind you, that

your uncle is much richer than your papa,
and, therefore, your aunt can afford with
propriety to do many things that I cannot."—
"Yes, I know she has a carriage and horses:
ah! I wish you were as rich, mamma."
"Thank you, my love; but I am very happy
with what I have, and I could only be happy
if I had more." Serena paused. "But,
mamma, when we see so many *richer* than
ourselves, we cannot help thinking"——"Of
how many are *poorer*," said her mother,
interrupting her. "But that I did not recollect just now."—"Yet now is the very
moment you ought to think of it: you are
not very rich, and therefore free from many
vexations attendant on money; you are not
poor, and therefore secured from the miseries
of want. Placed in a middle station, thank
God for the unembittered blessings He has
given you."—"Yet still, mamma, I cannot
think money brings care, as you say. Now

what care can there be in riding in a coach?"
—"I cannot enter more into the subject now,
Serena; and, therefore, only beg you will
exert your own sense. Observe what happens
around you. I may one day find you acknowledging, that even riding in a coach is not
always a pleasure."

CHAPTER III.

The Pleasures of Walking.—The Inconveniences of a Coach.—Change produced by Ill-humor.—Greediness punished.

EARLY the next morning, Serena sprang most joyfully from her bed: the sun was just beginning to beam; the robin redbreast was twittering its solitary, yet sweet, notes; all nature looked cheerful, and the heart of Serena danced with joy. Felix met his sister in the parlor, and they talk over the pleasures of the coming day.—They had each dressed themselves with the greatest neatness. Serena's frock was white as snow; her cheeks, just washed with clear cold water, bloomed like two roses; her hair was nicely combed, and hung in easy curls on her clean forehead, and her eyes sparkled with good humor. Felix,

as he kissed her, could not help thinking, that
all the fine clothes in the world would not
have made her look better than she now did.
Their kind parents indulged their eagerness,
and the breakfast appeared somewhat earlier
than usual. When it was over, Serena put on
her warm coat, and, her father taking her by
one hand, and Felix by the other, they set off
for the house of their grandfather.—The frost
had dried the roads, and hung glittering on
each spray. Felix often stopped to observe
the grass and leaves, that shone as if gemmed
by diamonds. The air breathed fresh, and,
though they had a mile to walk, they very soon
found themselves at their grandfather's door;
indeed, almost too soon, for they had discovered so much to admire—the ponds adorned
with fantastic piles of ice that spread out into
a variety of shapes, the boys skating on the sur-
face, the whistling of the distant woodman, the
stroke of his axe as its sound followed its sight

"Papa," said Felix, breathless with surprise, "how is it that we can see the blow, before we hear the sound? Both must happen together."—"Both do happen together; but sound travels so much slower than sight."— "Sound travel, papa!"—"Yes, my dear, the progress it makes, from the place whence it issues to our sense of hearing, I call travelling. Does not thunder follow lightning at a greater or less interval?"—"Yes, papa." —"Yet they are both emitted together. Thus, by the time that elapses between the thunder and the flash of lightning, its distance from us can be calculated. However, this subject is too difficult for you at present: and, besides, we are arrived at the end of our walk."

Grandpapa received his guests with his usual kindness and affection: scarcely were they seated by the blazing fire, when a handsome coach drew up to the door, and Felix saw his aunt and four cousins alight from it

Here were new greetings—every body was talking, and all was joy and hilarity. Serena, in the gaiety of her heart, described the beauty of their walk.—" Dear cousin, did not the ice look beautiful, like stars and spears, and I don't know what pretty things? And were not the leaves shining with a thousand diamonds? The grass, too, edged with such a silvery fringe !"

" Why, Serena," answered her cousin, " how could we see all these charming things ? You know we were boxed up in the coach."—" I had forgotten : but then you heard the birds singing; and, cousin, did you observe the woodman on the opposite side of the river ? I have something clever to tell you about him."—" How could I hear any thing but the rattling of the wheels ? " Serena was confounded ; she turned her eyes upon her father : he smiled, and, taking her hand, softly said, " You find, Serena, walking has some pleasures, which a coach cannot indulge." He then rose to return home, as his wife was alone and would expect him. "Do not send for your children," said their aunt : "I will see them both safely home in the coach."

This was a most welcome proposal to Felix and his sister, who, with added alacrity, bade adieu to their father, and now followed their cousins into a large room prepared for them. Here grandpapa distributed to each of them some new toys; then, bidding them to be merry, he left them till the dinner-hour. A scene of much merriment ensued; many games were played, many stories told, many songs sung. Now they danced, and now skipped; good humor reigned amongst them, and they were happy. By degrees, they began to tire; some complained of hunger, some of cold; ill humor was creeping into their hearts, and of course turned all their good to evil. The room was equally warm.

5

the toys equally pretty; yet the first appeared
uncomfortable, and the last were thrown by in
disgust. Felix could not help recalling the
words of his father, that much pleasure would
cease to please; and that in a mixture of
labor and amusement, there was the greatest
enjoyment of both: he also considered their
murmurs as highly ungrateful to their kind
grandfather, who had done so much to make
them happy. Very earnestly, therefore, he
endeavored to prevail on the little party to
resume their sports; with his sister, he quickly
succeeded; but his cousins were quarrelling
amongst themselves about their respective
toys. Felix offered to exchange his own with
them; Serena did the same: they were willing
to do any thing else their cousins chose. But
no—Felix found, to his sorrow, that, when
children are sullen and quarrelsome, nobody
can oblige them. Afraid of making them
worse, he drew Serena to the other side of

the room, and amused her and himself with a book, given him with the toys. The four cousins became more cross every minute: they scolded each other for what was the fault of all; and, at last, their passion made them so forgetful of themselves, that from words they proceeded to blows. What sight can be more shocking! Four brothers and sisters fighting and beating each other! Poor Serena turned pale with fear, and, throwing her arms round her brother, seemed to cling to him for protection. Felix tenderly kissed her; and, holding her firmly in his stouter arms, assured her nothing should hurt her. The noise of the combatants soon brought grandpapa to the field of action. When he entered the room, how was he affected!—On the four violent fighters he looked with anger and disgust; but the tender attitude of Felix and the trembling Serena melted him to tears of admiration; he fondly clasped them in his arms, and exclaim-

ed, "My own two dear children ! God bless
you ! God will bless you, for He looks down
with benignity on each family of love." The
mother of the rude quarrellers now appeared ;
how was she shocked, how did her heart ache,
when she viewed these four children, for whom
she had long felt an equal affection, whom she
had long beheld with equal anxiety, now distorted by rage, and vociferating with ill
humor! But we will not dwell on such a
frightful scene—convinced that our young
readers, with one voice, must resolve never
to give a cause of equal complaint to their
own parents ; but, like the affectionate Felix
and his sister, prove through life the comfort
and joy of all who love them, and the dearest
and firmest friends of each other. By the
friendly interference of Felix, his aunt was
prevailed upon to forgive this most distressing
outrage. His cousins were somewhat calmed :
but how different did every thing appear to

them now, from what it did when at first they gaily entered the play-room! In vain they declared everything was changed:—poor children! the only change was in their own hearts.

Dinner was announced, and the party sat down with excellent appetites. The beef and the plum-pudding were both highly extolled. Serena, indeed, found the latter so good, that she was just going to send her plate for a second slice of it, when Felix reminded her how rich it was, and, like a good sensible child, she immediately determined not to have any more. Her sense was here rewarded; for one of her cousins who would eat a great deal more, in spite of the admonitions of her mother, was taken so very sick, that she was obliged to be carried from table, and lay upon a bed most of the afternoon.—The rest drew round the cheerful fire, ate biscuits and apples, and heard some entertaining stories from their

5*

grandpapa. Tea now followed; and, soon after, the coach that was to convey them all home, drove up to the door. Felix and Serena had spent a most happy day; they loved their kind grandfather, yet they very cheerfully bade him good-b'ye; for they knew they were about to return to a happy home, where they should meet their affectionate parents; and, by describing all their past joys to them, would enjoy them a second time. With light hearts, therefore, they skipped into the carriage, their grandpapa calling out to them that they had been such well-behaved children, he should be very glad to see them again whenever they had leave to visit him.

The coach rattled merrily along. It was a dark night; and, as nothing could be seen, Serena did not regret being boxed up, as her cousins called it. At first, she was very merry; but by degrees her little tongue ceased to prate, and soon she was quite silent; she, however, did not complain, and her quietness passed unnoticed. In half an hour they reached home; for the carriage-road was much longer than the path across the fields. Felix sprang out of the coach, and found his parents at the door waiting for them; Serena slowly followed, and, both thanking their aunt, the coach proceeded home, and our little party entered the house. "We have had a charming day," exclaimed Felix; and he rapidly described their various pleasures, carefully avoiding only the account of his cousins' misbehavior. This, he knew, would pain his parents; besides, he remembered that excellent command in the Bible, "Do as you would be done by," and would not expose faults in another; assured that he himself often did things that wanted excusing.

Serena was all this time still, and often leaned her head on her hand. The eye of a mother is quick in watching the alterations in the looks of her child. Serena showed that she was ill, and her mother tenderly inquired what ailed her. " Indeed, mamma, I do not know, but my head aches. Oh! how it aches!"—"My poor girl! I fear you have eaten something that has disagreed with you." —"No, I did not; for, according to what you always desire, I dined on one meat dish, which was roast beef, and I took only one piece of pudding: besides, I am not at all sick."—"I think I know the cause," said her father; "it is the ride home."—".Ah! papa, I do think it was; for I was so merry when I got in, and presently everything seemed turning about, and I could not hear plainly, nor see plainly, and then this terrible pain came on."—"It is a very common effect, my dear; I know many people who are always sick and ill if they ride only a very short distance."—"Papa, little did I think a coach could give any pain."—"So it is, my love,

with us all. We wish for something we do
not possess, without considering whether it is
worth our wish. Perhaps, after many endeavors, we gain our wish. Then, it is only then,
we are convinced of its insufficiency to make
us happy. But I must not talk—it will hurt
your poor head."—"It is better already:
sitting still and holding it upon dear mamma's
shoulder, has almost cured it."—"That is a
proof, then, that it has really been occasioned
by the closeness and noise of the carriage;
however, you have had a long day, and had
better go to bed. Remember only never to
wish for any thing till you are perfectly assured it is really valuable; and even then it is
better to discover how we can be happy without it: so pray never wish again but for wisdom
and virtue."—"Indeed, papa, if I ever catch
myself wanting what I have not, I will remember the coach."—"Do so, my love: and now,
good night."—The recovered Serena and her

brother, after kissing their parents, retired to their chambers : there they knelt, and thanked a good God for the many blessings He had given them; and then, jumping into their own snug beds, soon fell into a sweet sleep.

CHAPTER IV.

Sorrow useless.—The Pleasures of School.—The Advantage of speaking Truth.—The best Reward for a good Action is Self-approval.

THE days were now becoming gradually longer. Serena watched their increase with sensations of mingled pain and pleasure ; for with the lengthened days Easter approached —Easter, that was to rob her of the society of her brother. Her mother observed her distress, and very kindly led her to different occupations ; assured that constant employment would not only stamp value on her time, but also draw her mind from the contemplation of the approaching separation. Serena was more industriously occupied in preparing for her brother's future comfort. His neat new handkerchiefs were of her

hemming; his silk purse she had netted; and
with her own hands she fresh-lined the deal
box that was to contain his books. How
much better was this active kindness, how
much more useful these proofs of her affection,
than if she had blinded herself with weeping,
or with sickly *sensibility* denied herself and all
around every source of pleasure!

The day at length arrived: Felix, with firm
yet affectionate heroism, prepared for his journey. The chaise was at the door: his father
waited. Serena, with an aching heart, vainly
endeavored to suppress her tears. Her mother
felt for her; but, knowing the mischiefs of
indulging in sorrow, she urged her to exert
herself.—"Come, my love," said she, "I
know you love your brother, I am sure you
do not wish to pain him."—"Indeed, I do
not," feebly articulated Serena. "Yet you
must be assured this grief must pain him:
rouse yourself Serena; let not your brother

recall your image clouded by this distress.
Let him only remember his happy smiling
Serena—your memory will then serve to cheer
and enliven him." Serena sprang from her
seat: her eyes still glistened with tears, but a
smile played on her lips; she made an effort
to check her sobs, and succeeded. "Good-
b'ye, Felix," she exclaimed with a cheerful
tone.—"We shall soon meet again," answered
Felix: "in less than three months!—Think
of that, Serena!"—"Oh! how joyful will be
our meeting!"—"My dear boy," said his
father, "it is thus that all our sweetest joys
must be purchased! We must pay for them
by some greater or less inconvenience."—
"But to part with those we love!" said
Serena. "It is painful I know, my dear;
but, after absence, to meet with those we
love!"—"That must be joy, indeed, papa."
—"That joy will, I trust, be one day yours;
but you must buy it by a present privation.—

6

Come, Felix, all is prepared." Felix hung a moment on Serena's neck, and her innocent tears wetted his glowing cheek. His mother fondly blessed him. Afraid of trusting himself any longer, he tore himself from their embraces, and rushed into the chaise, where his father was already seated—it instantly drove off.

As the view of his home disappeared, Felix sobbed aloud; and, overcome by his feelings, he threw himself into a corner of the carriage. For a few moments his father permitted him to remain unnoticed. He then took his hand, and said to him, "My dear boy, these tears are due to the most excellent of mothers and most affectionate of sisters. I would not have you part from them with indifference. So far from it, I would have you bear their remembrance incessantly in your heart. The recollection of their virtues will soften and improve your character, whilst the claims they have upon you will keep you steady in the pa* rectitude. Your name is theirs; do not therefore forget, that by staining your character you will also cloud theirs."—"Ah! papa, I hope I shall never dishonor either them or you."—"I anxiously hope not; but, as you are now going for the first time to stand alone to act from your own judgment, I must entreat you to think well how much depends on yourself. To your schoolfellows prove ever kind and obliging. Do not expose their faults, nor cause their punishment; it will be enough for you to guard your own conduct, and not disgrace yourself by being a spy on others. Keep strictly to truth. Let no disgrace, no entreaty, urge you in any one instance to be guilty of falsehood: a liar is the most contemptible of mortals! When you have done wrong, own it—instantly own it—acknowledge your fault, and be sorry for it. Take my word, such is the only honorable mode of behaving. What prevents a boy from con fessing he has done wrong?—A fear of punishment. Falsehood belongs only to *cowards*; they commit a fault, are afraid of correction, and try to hide it by a lie. A brave boy may be guilty of mischief, but he cannot be guilty of falsehood.—You, I hope, are no coward." —Felix's cheek glowed with an honest blush. "No, father, I hope I am neither a coward nor a liar!"—"Be careful, therefore, and prove your truth and your courage. You may be tried! and remember, I charge you, whatever temptations may arise, never conceal your faults;—and, after this warning, mark me, I will forgive any thing but a *lie!*"

Felix and his father travelled nearly the whole of the day; towards evening they reached the town where the school was situated. The master, a very worthy and sensible clergyman, received them with great kindness; he introduced Felix to his playfellows, who were numerous, amounting to more than a hundred. They gathered round Felix like so many bees ;—it will be strange, thought he, if, among so many, I shall not pick up two or three I shall like, and who will like me. His father spent the evening with the master, and, after an early supper, withdrew to the inn, whence he meant to set off homewards the next morning. Felix felt a pang as he saw him depart ; but, when he remembered how much he might please him by his improvement when next they met, he soon recovered himself, and, with tolerable composure, retired to the chamber allotted for him. Here he found a boy of nearly his own age expecting him, who kindly promised to teach him all their rules. Felix gratefully thanked him ; and, filling his mind with earnest resolutions of taking greatest pains to be all his father wished him to be, he quickly fell asleep.

Serena, in the meantime, was nearly overcome by the loss she had sustained of the society of her ever kind brother. Her mother, however, soon roused her, and reminded her of the pleasure of their hoped-for meeting.— "Ah! mamma, but that is so distant—three months, twelve weeks, what a long time!"— "Do not be calculating how long, my dear Serena, merely to distress yourself, but only think how the period had best be occupied: not in murmurings, surely."—"How then, mamma?"—"Why, suppose you endeavor to do something that will prove an agreeable surprise for your brother on his return?"— "What can I do, mamma?"—"Let me consider—what do you think of undertaking the care of his garden? The season is arrived when weeds grow rapidly, and will require constant attention. The young plants, as they increase, will need sticks to support them, the strawberry roots must be watered, and the rose-trees pruned."—"Thank you, dear mamma; this is a charming thought! how pleased Felix will be!—And may I also feed his favorite rabbit?"—"Yes; and now I think, you will have plenty of employment: time will not hang heavy on your hands; and Midsummer will be here before we think of it." Thus roused from her sorrow, Serena, with recovered smiles, entered on her various duties —amusements, I may say, for her parents made everything a pleasure to her, and, as she was neither obstinate nor sullen, it was easy to make her happy.

Felix was soon acquainted with his play-fellows. He found his master somewhat stern, but yet so reasonable in all his commands, that he felt he could not disobey him. Although not a remarkably clever boy, as we have already said, yet, by steadiness and perseverance, Felix made a rapid progress in his learning. His attention gained the good opinion of his master, and his obliging disposition secured him the love of the boys. School soon became very pleasant to Felix; and, though he often thought of home, he ceased to regret his absence from it.

One day he heedlessly threw a ball against a window. A pane of glass was smashed in pieces. "How unlucky!" said one of the boys; "but, never mind, I'll keep the secret; no one else is here, and, if inquiry be made, you can say the cat did it."—"I can say no such thing," replied Felix, "for that would be a lie."—"If it is known," continued the boy. "you must pay two shillings for the glass, and perhaps be flogged into the bargain."—"I will not tell a lie to save me from twenty floggings. I have already done wrong, and must have courage to bear my punishment."—"Do not say I was with you then, Master Courage," said the boy sneeringly. "Be not afraid," answered Felix: "I will not expose you to any blame." He then turned towards the

Felix and the Schoolmaster.

house, that he might have an opportunity of seeing his master. It was some time before this occured : at last he saw him coming out of his parlor, and modestly approached him. "What do you want, Felix?" said his master, a little sternly, at least Felix thought so ; but, though his heart beat quickly, he was a boy of true courage, and never feared to do his duty. "I am afraid," said he, in a timid voice, "I am afraid, sir, I have done very wrong ; but I hope you will forgive me."— "What have you done?" cried his master, in an angry tone. "I have very carelessly broken a pane of glass in the school-room window," answered Felix: "I was playing with a ball there."—"That is against the rules," said the master ; "you must pay the value of it." Felix produced his purse, and paid the two shillings.—"Do not let this happen again," continued the master, in a kinder tone ; "I excuse you from further

punishment, because you have so honorably
acknowledged your fault."—Felix bowed, and
with a lightened heart sprang away to his
business. It was true, he had thus lost two
shillings, and he was not very rich; but by
his honesty he had gained the good opinion
of his discerning master, who ever after this
accident was observed to treat him with peculiar kindness.—The elder boys also began
now to notice him, and were so much pleased
with this instance of his spirit, that they often
admitted him into their parties. This was a
great gratification to Felix, for he always
preferred the society of boys older than
himself, as from them he expected to gain
information.

Soon after this event, another occurred,
which threatened to be attended with more
serious consequences. One fine evening, some
of the boys had leave to take a walk; but
they were ordered not to go beyond a certain

distance, and to return at a certain hour.
Forth they joyfully sallied, Felix in the
number, and, traversing some beautiful fields,
came at last to the river. Here a few of the
party proposed bathing; but this was opposed
by the rest, as contrary to all rule. Felix
was one who peremptorily refused, although
particularly fond of the amusement. One of
the boys sneeringly told him he was afraid of
the water; another, that he dreaded the
flogging attendant on this breach of the law.
Felix only laughed at them; and, having in
vain attempted to persuade them, strolled into
a neighboring wood that skirted the river, and,
in search of wild flowers, soon lost sight of his
companions. After rambling about some time,
he sat down to rest himself, and form his
flowers into a nosegay. As he was thus
occupied, a distant shriek struck his ear—
another succeeded—he threw down his flowers, and rushed forwards, directed by the

sound : in a few seconds he found himself at
the edge of the river, and beheld one of the
boys vainly endeavoring to reach the bank—
he seemed exhausted and faint. Felix, with
a happy presence of mind, drew a long pole
from the hedge, and, holding one end firmly
himself, presented the other to his sinking
playmate. A reed can save a drowning man.
The boy caught the offered help, and was
thus easily drawn on shore. Felix supported
his dripping comrade to a bank, and then flew
in search of his clothes. These were left at
some distance farther up the river. Felix at
length found them ; and, though he made all
the haste in his power, much time was spent.
His companions hallooed out that they were
going home. Felix would not leave the poor
half-drowned boy, who looked piteously upon
him. In assisting him to dress, he wetted his
own clothes ; and, having used his handkerchief as a towel to dry his shivering com-

panion, he returned it, soaked with water, into his pocket.—" What will become of me!" said the frightened boy; " what will become of me! I shall certainly be flogged, I that am already half dead with fear and fatigue."—" Do not be so alarmed," said Felix; " I will do all I can to excuse you."—" Dear Felix, do not say I have been in the water." Felix shook his head. " But, do you know, I had not leave to be of the party?" continued the boy. —" Indeed!" exclaimed Felix; and he thought, but he did not speak his thought, how one fault leads to another.—" So, Felix, if you will keep my secret, I can, perhaps, get unobserved into the house," added the boy. " See how pale I am—how sick!—save me from punishment!" Felix looked compassionately upon him. " If it is in my power, I will save you."—" Then do not mention me."—" Not unless I am asked."— " Do you promise that?"—" I do." And

7

they began slowly to return homewards. The rest of the boys had reached the school; their bathing, in disobedince of all order, had been discovered, as all faults must be sooner or later. The master instantly punished every one who had been in the water The name of the absent Felix was resounding through the play-ground, as pale and dejected he entered the gates. His companion was a few steps behind, and, taking advantage of the confusion that reigned around, waited some minutes, then slipped in unobserved, and crept up to his chamber.

Felix, with a palpitating heart, obeyed the summons of his master. As he approached the school-room, he heard of the severity with which the disobedient boys had been treated. His master looked sternly upon him. "You, sir, to disobedience have added insolence, for you are nearly an hour beyond your appointed time." Felix could only feebly articulate, "I have not been in the water."—" How, then, comes your dress so wet?" Felix drew out his handkerchief to conceal his tears. Its dripping condition attracted the master's eye. He held it up in his hand. " If Felix himself has not been in the water, which of you has used this handkerchief? It has evidently served the purpose of a towel. Which of you has so used it?"—" Not I," was repeated from every mouth. The master turned again to Felix. "Recollect yourself," said he: "are you very sure you have not been in the water?"—"I am very sure, sir."—" Perhaps he washed his hands," said one of the ushers, kindly wishing to excuse him.—" Did you wash your hands?" asked the master. Here was an opportunity for Felix to have escaped, but it would have been by equivocation, a crime equal to a lie; he scorned such an unworthy refuge, and replied with a firm but modest tone, " No, sir, I did not wash

my hands."—"How then came your handkerchief so wet?" Felix deeply blushed.
"If you command, sir, I know I must tell you
—but pray, pray, sir, excuse me—do not
command me."—"This is very extraordinary," said the master; "why cannot you
answer me?"—"Because, sir"——— and his
voice faltered: "forgive me, but I have
promised"——— A murmur of applause sound
ed through the circle of boys. The excellent
and sensible master continued:—"Your for-
mer truth and candor lead me to believe you
now, Felix: as a proof of my regard, I will
not command you to speak now." Felix
bowed his thanks, for his heart was so full of
gratitude, that he could not speak. "I give
you, however," said his master, "the same
task, for having out-stayed your allotted time,
as I have given the other boys, who have, like
you, been truants." Felix respectfully took
his lesson, and with great diligence learned it.

His schoolfellows treated him with new marks of esteem ; and not a few reminded him of the advantage of having established a character for truth. It had saved him not only from disgrace, but also from punishment.

Some days after this, the real fact began to be rumored in the school, the boy himself having whispered it to his intimates. Felix appeared with added honor; all loved the kind-hearted boy, who, at the risk of himself, had saved his fellow. The secret by degrees reached the master's ear ; and, though he took no particular notice of it, yet Felix could observe that he was ever after a great favorite with his master, being treated with many proofs of kindness and distinction.—" I do not think," said one of the boys to Felix, " I do not think you have got much for your good temper and forbearance."—" Then you know nothing about the matter," answered Felix ; " I have got all that I expected."—" And

7*

what may that be?" asked the boy. "A self-approving conscience," replied Felix. "Besides, is not my master kinder to me, and are not all you boys more obliging? What more could I expect?"—"Well, you are a fine fellow; but, as they say virtue is always rewarded, I should have expected some great good for my great virtue."— "Pshaw! Nonsense! In the first place, I do not think I have performed any *great* virtue; and, in the second place, as there are now no fairies," added Felix, laughing, "I did not suppose I should find either Fortunatus's purse, or Sinbad's valley of diamonds!"

CHAPTER V.

Money only valuable according as it is used.—Stinginess
described.—Perseverance conquers great Difficulties.—
The Nobleness of acknowledging an Error.—Returning
Good for Evil, the only Christian Revenge.

THE observation with which the last chapter
concluded was a very proper one, and ought
to be remembered. By the rewards that
follow good actions, is meant that self-satis-
faction which our own heart bestows; and
people would be very silly if they were always
expecting some wonderful benefits to follow
their just actions. Besides, if they did so,
they would destroy the merit of what they
had done. What virtue is there in performing
an act for which a full return is expected?
No; we must do all the good we can, from a
sense of duty; and if it please God to make

our own breasts reward us, by a secret whisper
that we have done well, we shall be paid
beyond all worldly praise.

The father of Felix, as I said before, was
not a rich man, but he made his son a regular
allowance of pocket-money ; which, though
much less than most of the other boys had,
Felix managed so well, that it supplied him
with all he wanted.

Going once into his bed-room for something
he had left there, he was surprised to observe
a boy in the corner of the room ; but, knowing
it was wrong to pry into what others were
doing, he turned his head another way. It
was a rule that no boy should visit his room
in the day, except to fetch any thing : Felix,
therefore, was hastily returning with what he
had come for, when the boy called him back.
"Felix, do not tell what I was about."—
"I did not see what you were about."—
"Not see ! not hear my money ?"—"No."—

"Well, then, step here, and I will show you how rich I am." Felix approached him, and perceived a little heap of money—sixpences, shillings, and crowns. "You lucky boy! how did you get all this cash?"—"Saved it, to be sure. This is all I have received this last half-year."—"And what have you saved it for?" The boy looked confused. "Saved it!—why," and he stammered, "to keep it, to be sure." Felix laughed heartily: "Saved it to keep it!" repeated he: "what a valuable use of money!"—"Why," said the boy, "what can I do better?"—"Spend it, to be sure."—"Spend it! No, indeed; if I had spent it as I got it, how do you think I could now have had all this treasure?"—"Don't call it a treasure," cried Felix; "it is rather a plague, I think."—"Why, yes, to be sure, it does make me uneasy sometimes; for I am afraid of losing it."—"Oh! pray do not be afraid of that; if you do lose it, it will not

signify." The boy looked aghast. " Not
signify ! " said he breathlessly. " No, certainly ; if you do not spend it now, nor intend
to spend it by and by, pray would not copper
counters be as well as this good money?
Come, I will rid you of all this trouble at
once ; give me the money, and, like the man
in the fable, I will give you a famous bag of
stones. This no one will rob you of, and
you will be freed from all anxiety." So
saying, and laughing as he spoke, Felix left
this unhappy little miser, feeling for him a
mingled sentiment of pity and contempt.

Not long after this, an annual fair occurred.
The boys were allowed to attend it : the
younger under the care of the ushers ; the
elder in small parties of ten or a dozen.
Felix, amongst the rest, issued joyfully from
the school gates, and enjoyed all the various
sports of the scene. The jostling of the
crowd took something from his pleasure, and

Felix at the Fair Ground.

a good deal confused him. "Ah!" thought he, "this is not so pleasant as a fine scamper in the open fields. Here, I can scarcely creep along; and the noise is so great it almost makes my head ache! I am glad a fair does not come often; and a walk in the country is always in our power. The best joys, I think, are the easiest to be had!" Felix thought very properly: a good God, in placing us in this world, intended us to be happy in it, and graciously contrived that every true pleasure should be easiest to be attained.

If my young readers will stop for a moment, and think of this, they will find it is indeed so.

Felix had not forgotten to put his purse into his pocket; he now produced it, and bought a very neat red morocco housewife for his sister. It was well stored with needles and thread, and contained, besides, a small pair of scissors. This purchase made, he next laid out some money on a paper of gingerbread,

part of which he gave to·the boy he walked
with. They continued strolling along, and
arrived at a very smart stall, adorned with
every kind of cutlery. Some handsome knives
looked very tempting: one was presented to
him as particularly good. Felix looked at it;
it was certainly very complete: "What was
the price?" The man informed him; the
sum was very little less than the whole contents of his purse. "It is too dear," said
Felix, putting it down; show me one cheaper."
His companion exclaimed, "You are a stingy
dog! I will have the knife, although it will
cost me all my remaining cash." Felix only
laughed; he knew he was not stingy, and was
determined to keep steady to his original
intention. Just let it be observed here, that
children should never be *laughed* out of their
resolutions; for that shows a weak and silly
mind. The boy bought the handsome knife,
and laid out all his money. Felix chose a

cheaper one, but strong and equally useful;
and by this means saved two shillings. "You
do not want those two shillings," said his
companion. "I do not at this moment, but I
may by and by," answered Felix; and they
walked on. A variety of amusements occupied their attention, and, highly entertained,
the time slipped insensibly away. "Let us
remember our hour," said Felix, and drew his
companion towards a respectable shop, the
master of which very obligingly informed them
what o'clock it was. "Let us go home,"
cried Felix. "It wants half an hour to our
time," said the boy. "We shall spend that
half hour in getting along; the crowds prevent
our moving quick." Felix was firm to his
decision, and his friend consented. They
turned homewards, and had not proceeded far,
when they were arrested by a group of people.
They pushed among them, and found a poor
black man, lame, and covered with rags,

recounting his story, and asking charity. The
hand of Felix was instantly in .his pocket.
" You will not give your money to a common
street beggar?" said his companion. " No,
not to common street beggars, because I
believe they are generally idle cheats: but
this is no common beggar; he is a stranger,
distant from his native land, and without
friends; disabled too from working. I will
share the contents of my purse with him: "
so saying, Felix presented a shilling to the
poor cripple, who blessed the generous English
boy. " Ah! massa, if all your countrymen
were like you, I should not be here a poor,
despised, helpless beggar!" This appeal
softened the hearts of many of his hearers;
they followed the example of Felix, and, as
he withdrew, he had the secret joy of feeling
he had not only himself assisted a suffering
fellow-creature, but had led others to do so
too. His companion walked sorrowfully along.

"This Felix stingy!" thought he; "ah! he is truly generous. I wish I had not spent all my money so idly." Felix was also silent; but his looks were so gay, his heart so happy, his step so light! His knife, too, that plain, unadorned knife, was a source of one of his sweetest recollections. He never cut a stick, nor mended a pen, but the thought of the black man rushed into his mind; and he always loved his cheap knife, which, by saving his money, had given him the power of being charitable.

It has been already said, that Felix was not a remarkably clever boy; his lessons often appeared very difficult to him. By great patience and perseverance he had conquered these difficulties. One day, however, he had a Latin lesson to learn which very much puzzled him. He almost cried as he read it, but, knowing this would not do him any good, he wiped away his half-formed tears, and

again set to learn his book ; again it baffled
his exertion. Assured that it *must* be learnt,
he began to consider what he had best do ·
he thought, if he could prevail upon some one
to read it over to him and explain it, he could
more easily learn it. Thus determined, he
took up his book, and with a melancholy air
approached one of the ushers. " What makes
you look so sad, Felix ? " said the usher,
" you, that are always so merry and contented."—" Sir," said Felix, very respectfully,
" my Latin lesson for to-day has quite puzzled
me ; will you be so kind as to explain it to
me ? "—" That I will, readily," answered the
good-natured usher ; and, taking the book,
he showed Felix where he had made some
mistakes. " Thank you, sir," said Felix ;
" though it is still very difficult, yet now I
believe I can master it."—" That I do not
doubt," replied the usher ; " but, suppose I
had not been here, what would you have

done ?" Felix considered a little, and then said, "Asked one of the elder boys."—"But they might have been too busy; and your lesson must be learnt."—"I think, then," said Felix, "I should have begun all over again, and tried, and tried, till I had discovered my blunders."—"You would then have done right, Felix," said the usher; "and, by taking such means, be assured you can conquer greater difficulties than this. Never forget, that by patience and perseverance all knowledge is attained; and, without these, the cleverest boy in the school can never make any progress." Felix bowed, and retired. With renewed attention he took up his book; by degrees all difficulty vanished; and, before the school hour, he was prepared with his lesson. Thus, though a boy of very moderate talents, he made a daily progress in all useful knowledge, and was respected by the elder boys. The younger loved him sincerely, for

he was so ready to please and oblige them.
He always, however, took care to choose his
friends from amongst the elder and superior
boys of the school, as he not only preferred
their company, but he thought it would do
him good, as, being more clever than himself,
their conversation would improve him, and
their superior characters would be useful exam-
ples for him to copy.   Felix would not have
been admitted as a playfellow to the higher
classes if he had not gained, by his good
behavior, a respectable name in the school.
When the boys found that he was never guilty
of a lie ; that he was not a miser; that he
never performed mean actions : never told tales
either to the master or ushers ; they began to
esteem him, and very readily admitted him
among them.

Felix was happy in a very noble way of
thinking; and, as all stories of spirited behavior are generally admired by children, they

shall now hear one of true spirit.—Felix dined out, one day, with one of the day scholars; many other boys were also there, and several ladies and gentlemen. The party was large: they sat down to an excellent dinner, and were all very merry. Felix and a younger boy, who sat opposite to him at table, entered into dispute about something that had happened the day before. No one had been present at the circumstance but themselves; each was positive in his own opinion; at length, the eyes of the company were drawn upon them, and they seemed disposed to believe that Felix, as being the elder, was more likely to be right. At last, the little boy remembered a particular circumstance, which till then they had both forgotten. This was decisive. Felix blushed for having been so positive, and instantly exclaimed to the little boy,—"You are right, and I am wrong. I remember it all now, and beg your

pardon."—"What a noble boy!" said most
of the company; "with what true spirit he
acknowledges his mistakes! with what true
spirit asks pardon for them!" To do wrong,
is common; to acknowledge it, is the virtue
of a superior mind.

Another time Felix showed the great command he had gained over his faults, for he had
faults; and, if he had not conquered them, he
never would have been the superior character
he now appeared. The boys were all playing
in parties on the play-ground: Felix had a
favorite bat and trap which his father had
given him: in the course of the game, one of
the boys was often vanquished by Felix; this
made him angry; he became passionate; and,
seizing the favorite bat and trap of Felix, he
cried, " I will be avenged!" and instantly
shattered them both to pieces. Felix, vexed
and mortified, had nearly lost his patience;
but happily recovering himself, he calmly

said, "If you are so ungovernable, I will not play with you," and walked away. Some days afterwards, another of the boys, by chance, obtained the passionate boy's bat and trap; he instantly took them to Felix, and, presenting them, told him this was a charming opportunity for avenging himself. "It is indeed," said Felix. The boy waited to see the bat and trap destroyed. Felix continued, " Do you give me these? May I do what I please with them?"—"Certainly," answered the boy. " Then," said Felix, "I will show you what I will do with them;" and, taking the bat and trap in his hand, he ran up to the passionate boy, who was searching for them about the play-ground:—" Here," cried Felix, " here are your bat and trap!" The passionate boy looked surprised:—" Have not you broken them?"—" Broken them!" exclaimed Felix; " no, I should be ashamed to have done that; they are quite safe—take them—let us be friends again—for now I am avenged." Felix good-humoredly held out his hand. The passionate boy eagerly seized it:—"Ah, you have returned good for my evil."

This same passionate boy was under another obligation to Felix. The master, one day, discovered that one of the most valuable school books had been greatly injured. The book had been lent to this boy; and his master, sending for him, very severely reprimanded him for his carelessness; and, as the book was stained with many blots of ink, the boy had a long task given him. Felix heard the whole of this affair, and stepping up to the master, he modestly said, "Sir, I am afraid I have been guilty of this mischief."—"You! how could you have done it?"—"I came into the school-room, last night, to put away my ink-bottle: it was dark, I had no candle, and felt my way by the stools and forms; in moving along, I stumbled against something, which I found at the moment had shaken some ink out of my bottle; but, the usher calling me to go to bed, I did not wait to pick up what was in my way, which I fancy, sir, was this book." The master was silent a moment; then said, "I think it is very probable that what you say has been the case."—"As it was my fault, may this boy be excused?"—"He had no business to leave the book carelessly on the floor: however, I will excuse him, and let him thank you; your frankness has saved him."

CHAPTER VI.

Accuracy in Spelling essential to Writing.—Accuracy in Language essential to Truth.—Patience in Sickness and Pain.—Time found for every useful Business.--The Evils of Procrastination.—Dreams.

SERENA, deeply occupied with her various avocations, thought of Felix with mingled sensations of joy and hope. In feeding his rabbits, and arranging his garden, she felt she was preparing a pleasure for her dear brother. As she was fond of writing, she wished to send him a letter every week, but her mother would not permit her. "Why not, mamma?" said Serena. "Because, my love, it is getting into a bad habit, to be always scribbling ; and I fancy Felix will depend upon your loving him, and thinking of him, without your being obliged to tell him so every week."—" But.

mamma, I do so love writing!"—"And do you think, little girl, you can write so well, or spell so correctly, as to render letter-writing easy to you?"—"I can spell tolerably, mamma; I seldom make mistakes, only one letter here or there."—"And do you not know that even one false or misplaced letter will entirely alter the meaning of a word, sometimes of a whole sentence?"—"How can that be, mamma?"—"I will tell you. Suppose you wished to inform your brother that the chief magistrate, the mayor of our town, called here last week, and you were to write, 'the *mare* was here a few days since;' this would be making it appear that an animal, not a man, was the subject of your letter. Thus again, if, wishing to describe the young hare, which your papa gave you yesterday, you were to say, 'my *hair* grows very pretty, and will, I think, be a beautiful brown'—what would your brother imagine, but that his little

Serena was grown vain, and was boasting of
her curls!"—"Ah! mamma, I understand;
how ridiculous would be such mistakes!"—
"And yet they are very slight, though so
important in their effects.　Judge, therefore,
of what consequence is a close attention to
accuracy in spelling; and, before you attempt
to write, learn perfectly how to spell."—
"Mamma, what do you mean by that hard
word *accuracy?*"—"I mean nicety, exact-
ness, without defect; accuracy in spelling
denotes that every word is correctly lettered,
there not being one letter too much, nor one
too little, nor one misplaced."—"Thank you,
mamma, I understand: but sometimes you
say, 'Be accurate in speaking'—that has
nothing to do with letters."—"No, my love,
that implies rather the use of words than
letters.　For instance, when you say you are
ready to die with the heat, you are not
accurate; you use a wrong word: you well

know you are not likely to die; and you would be correct to say, you are faint or exhausted with heat."—"Oh! yes, I see now."

"This inaccuracy of speech is not simply inelegant, Serena; it is often highly faulty."—"Indeed, mamma! How can that be?"—"Why, in describing the actions of our acquaintance, a trifling inattention may produce serious consequences. Thus, I once heard an otherwise well-meaning woman speak of a neighbor of hers as the stingiest creature in the world; when, in fact, her neighbor, as she well knew, had so small an income that she was obliged to use the greatest possible care in her expenditure."—"What should she have said, mamma?"—"Had she called her neighbor very prudent, very economical, she had been accurate; but by using the expression 'very stingy,' she gave an unfavorable impression of her neighbor's character."—

" That was very ill-natured, mamma "—" I
do not imagine it was intended to be so, my
dear; but this lady had long indulged herself
in a great latitude of speech, and used words
without considering the full extent of their
meaning. Thus, when she tells me she is in
an *agony* of pain in her head, I simply understand that she has a head-ache; or, when she
declares she had not a wink of sleep all night,
I merely imagine she did not sleep as much
as usual: so you see that these inaccurate
speakers lose themselves very much in the
estimation of others."—" Mamma, I will always try to speak correctly."—" Do so, my
love! By such an endeavor you will acquire
a habit of precision, which will attend you
through life, and give a consequence to all
you utter."

Not very long after this conversation Serena
became much indisposed; her disorder was
the measles; she was very ill, and for some

time it was doubtful whether her life could be
saved.   Now it was that this little girl felt all
the happiness of possessing a kind and affectionate mother.   If, after a slight doze, she
drew aside her bed-curtains, what did she
behold?   Her mother, her watchful mother,
sitting by her, silent and motionless!—Who
held her throbbing temple?   Who hung over
her midnight slumbers?   Her never-wearied
mother!—" Ah!" thought she, "can I ever
repay all this kindness, this patience, this
forbearance?"   She turned her eyes upon her
mother, who, pale and wearied, sat still beside
her.   "Dear mamma, go to bed, pray go to
bed; you see I am better."—"My child!"
said her mother, instantly assuming a look of
cheerfulness, "I thank God that you are
better; it rewards me for all my anxiety."
The tears filled Serena's eyes.   "Ah! mamma, but all this watching!   I fear it has made
you ill!"—"No, my dear Serena, I am not

ill ! I am only a little sleepy ; but this is the
hour for taking your medicine, I will give it to
you." She arose and prepared the medicine.
Serena took the cup, and, though the contents
were nauseous, instantly drank off the draught.
Her mother smiled, and said, " You are a
good child, you take physic well."—" Oh !
mamma, I should be very wicked, if I were to
add to your trouble, and be perverse. How
easy for me to take a few mouthfuls of physic ;
whilst you, night and day, pass your life in
this dull room, and scarcely eat or drink !—.
Mamma, shall I ever forget this ? Can I ever
cease to remember what you have done for
me ?"—" I am sure my Serena will repay all
my cares, and prove ever gentle, ever affectionate. But we must not talk ; the doctor
will soon be here and scold us, for he bade us
keep you quiet." The doctor came, he found
Serena better; she gradually recovered, and
in another week was able to come down

stairs. Her mother, however, continued thin and dejected. Sometimes Serena thought she looked as if in pain; but, when this was observed, her mother always smiled off her fears. At length Serena was perfectly recovered; her eye was again bright; her cheek again rosy. She bounded with joy over the fresh lawn; she felt the value of existence, the charm of recovered health. " I never thought," said she, " how happy it was to be strong before! How charming it is to breathe this fresh air, to smell these sweet flowers, to listen to the warbling birds! If I had not been sick, I should not have tasted all the pleasures of health."—" True, Serena," said her father; " be grateful, then, for the recovered blessing; thank a good God, who has restored you to health and enjoyment."— " I do, papa! I do!" cried Serena, as she turned her eyes to heaven; whilst her little heart breathed a prayer of ardent gratitude.

Her father folded her clasped hands in his, and joined in the silent ejaculation.

" But, mamma," said Serena, first recovering herself, " mamma is, I fear, ill."—" She has sprained her arm, my dear," said her father tenderly ; " but it is getting better,—it will soon be well."—" Sprained her arm ! " repeated Serena sorrowfully ; " when did that happen ? "—" In your illness."—" Yes, I dare say, with holding me so many hours : but she never complained."—" No, my love, it would have grieved you ; your mother *seldom* thinks of herself,—*never* when another is to be thought of."—" How good she is, how very good ! "—" She has a firm mind, Serena, which conquers self, and makes her feel only for others. Copy her fortitude, my dear child ; fortitude will give value to all your other virtues." Her mother now approached ; Serena threw herself into her arms, and sobbed out her love,—her gratitude. Her parents tenderly embraced her. It was a happy scene! such as we all have in turn felt, but which we can never properly describe. Serena now became the nurse, and with daily care attended to her mother—the sprained arm was restored by her good nursing. How happy did she feel when rubbing it in the morning, when watching and aiding it through the day! Her mother had but to look, and the prompt Serena executed the unexpressed command. What a blessing to be useful to those we love! Serena felt this every day, and every day saw her happy and contented. Her mother was again well. Serena again took her accustomed seat by her side, and produced her work, " Mamma, I should very much like to knit Felix a pair of worsted socks: you have taught me to knit, you know, and I think I could do them!"—" By all means, then, my love, begin them!"—" But, mamma, I have no time; you see I have as nuch to do in the day as I can possibly get through."—"Still I think you could accomplish this matter, without neglecting any other duty."—"How, mamma?"—"At what hour do you rise in the morning, Serena?"—"Soon after seven, mamma."—"The sun is up much earlier than that?"—"Oh, yes! the sun now rises at four."—"Suppose, then, you were to get up at six instead of seven?"—"That would only give me one hour."—"How long does it want to the holidays?"—"Six weeks, mamma—and there are six working-days in a week:—an hour a-day would be six hours a-week—six hours a-week for six weeks would be thirty-six hours, mamma. I wonder I did not think of that before."—"You find, Serena, how easy it is to contrive to find time for whatever we really wish to do; by arranging our hours for every day, we discover what we are capable of undertaking; thus, with a little reflection and a little calculation, you have

made yourself the possessor of thirty-six unoc-
cupied hours."—" You found it out for me
mamma ; I could not think of any other way
but that of putting off my French or needlework."—" That would not have been a good
plan, Serena."—" No, mamma, this is much
better."

Serena kept her resolution ; she regularly
rose at six ; the socks rapidly proceeded ; and
Serena used to laugh and say, that she now
knew even how to make time.

We have already said that this little girl
had faults ; one of them was an idle habit
of postponing, putting off any business that
ought to be done to-day until to-morrow.—
To-morrow arrived, and brought its own occupations ; again Serena postponed, and again
found that opportunity lost cannot be recalled.
" My dear Serena," said her mother, one
morning, " have you fed the rabbits ? "—" No,
mamma, but I intend to do it by and by,"

replied Serena.—" Why by and by, Serena?
Why not do it now?"—" Because, because,
mamma,"—and she hesitated. " You are at
leisure now!"—" Yes, I know, mamma, but"
——" But what, Serena? You know it must
be done; and what time better than the
present?"—" Oh! just now I intended to go
into my garden."—" Is that necessary?"—
" No, mamma, not at all necessary; only
for pleasure."—" Then you set aside a
positive duty for a pleasure: is that right,
Serena?"—" Indeed, mamma, I will not
forget the rabbits."—" Well, my dear, act
by your own judgment, I have already given
you my opinion." Serena stood a few
moments uncertain what to do: at length, she
thought she would take a short peep at her
garden, and there still would be time to feed
her rabbits. She went to the garden, tied up
a carnation, weeded the mignonette bed, and
was so deeply engaged, that she forgot time

would not stay for her.—Dinner hour arrived :
after dinner, a walk was proposed by her
father; Serena joyfully accompanied them;
she returned just time enough to eat her
supper, attend to her evening lesson, and then
retired to bed. No sooner, however, had she
laid her head upon her pillow, then she began
recalling the events of the day. The poor
starving rabbits! The remembrance struck
to her heart—but it was now too late : at
such an hour they could not be fed. " They
will all be dead in the morning," thought
Serena. "What a cruel girl I have been!
Had I taken mamma's advice—Oh! I think,
I am *sure*, I will never put off any necessary
business again for pleasure." With such
thoughts Serena tormented herself for some
hours : at last she fell asleep, but her dreams
continued her waking thoughts. The rabbits,
continued to harass her, and she awoke early,
unrefreshed by her slumbers. The sun was

shining brightly; it was six o'clock Serena
hastily arose, dressed herself, and crept gently
down stairs. With a trembling hand she filled
her small basket with lettuces and parsley,
and then hastened to her rabbits. With joy
she beheld the two old ones run towards her;
they pressed through the pales of their box,
and greedily devoured the offered food. " But
the two young ones—where are they ? " exclaimed Serena : " I have lost my two pretty
little rabbits ! "—One of the maids heard her
lamentations.   " What is the matter, miss ? "
said she, approaching her.   " My young rabbits," cried Serena, " they are gone."—The
maid examined the box.—" I do not see how
they could go," said she : " it is certainly
impossible. You are so attentive, miss, or I
should have thought "——" What would you
have thought ? " exclaimed Serena. " Why,
miss, that the old ones had been hungry, and
eaten their young." Serena shuddered. " Do

not say so," she cried; "pray do not say so: how shocking! how wicked!"—"It is a common case, miss, when rabbits are not well watched; but as that cannot have happened now"——"Oh! yes, yes, it has happened," cried Serena; "I have neglected them—and now I am punished for it." The maid looked surprised. Serena resolved not to add another fault to the one she had already committed. "The socks," thought she, "shall not be neglected; and as for the rabbits, I will tell Felix the truth, and he, I hope, will forgive me."

At breakfast Serena told her parents what had happened. Her father was much displeased; her mother greatly lamented the sad effects of procrastination. "Well may procrastination be called the thief of time," said she, addressing Serena; "but I hope this will be a lesson to you, never to put off till tomorrow what may be done to-day."—"In-

10*

deed, mamma, I will take care in future to do
every thing in its place, and not neglect a
duty for a pleasure,—I ought not to say
pleasure, for I have had a great deal of pain—
all night I dreamed of my poor rabbits,
mamma; was not that strange?"—"No, my
dear, dreaming is only a kind of thinking;
and, if your mind has been engrossed with
any particular subject during the day, it seems
natural that the same image should occupy
your thoughts in sleep."—"Mamma, this
seems all very simple; but dreams, I thought,
were something wonderful?"—"The vulgar
and uninformed think so, and contrive, very
often, to frighten themselves; but people who
think properly, consider dreams, as I have told
you, only sleeping fancies."—"But, mamma,
I have heard of dreams coming true."—"We
may certainly so twist about dreams, and so
interpret them, as to make them appear
ominous; but this is the weakness of feeble

minds.   My Serena, I nope, will indulge
more useful thoughts."—"Yet, mamma, some
dreams are very frightful."—"When people
go to bed, Serena, with full stomachs, with
disordered heads, or fatigued bodies, the mind,
confused and agitated, is apt to produce wild
and distorted images: but surely there is
nothing miraculous in this."—"No, not as
you account for it, mamma.   Yet is not the
night-mare something very shocking?"—"The
night-mare, Serena, is only a name for an
oppression on the chest, produced by indi-
gestion, an awkward position of the head and
neck, or some such cause."—"Ah! mamma,
how easy that is to understand!—I shall
never mind dreams again."—"You are right,
my dear; let me also beg you will not repeat
them.   I do not know anything more silly or
fatiguing than the tedious account of dreams.
Do you remember that hymn of Watts's,
Serena?"—"Yes, indeed I do, mamma:—

'He told me his dreams, talk'd of eating and drinking.
But scarce reads his Bible, and never loves thinking.'"

" In these lines you find the describing of dreams is considered as one of the follies of a sluggard—an idle, consequently an useless, mortal! Never cease to repeat and consider the useful caution. But breakfast is over; bring your books, and let us begin our studies."

CHAPTER VII.

Obedience a Virtue.—Vexation most frequently produced by ourselves.—Happiness or Sorrow springs from our Hearts.

GRANDPAPA sent another kind invitation; Serena was allowed to accept it, and with a joyful heart attended the summons. She found her grandfather alone; he was not very well, and had wished for the company of the cheerful Serena; he thought it would do him good. Serena was delighted with the hope of cheering her kind grandfather; she brought a stool close to him, and told him all the prettiest stories she could remember; she read to him out of her last new book, then repeated some hymns, and was so eager to please him, that he was quite surprised when the dinner-hour arrived, not thinking it near so late. He

kissed and thanked his affectionate little enter-
tainer. What a reward for Serena, to have
pleased one who had so often conduced to her
pleasure ; to have soothed the heavy hour of
pain, and enlivened the gloom of sickness!
The dinner consisted of many good things,
and grandpapa, with great kindness, pressed
his visitor to eat of them all. But Serena,
though alone, and acting for herself, knew
what was proper to do—not only knew it, but
did it. She dined on some boiled mutton and
potatoes, and afterwards ate one piece of
gooseberry-pie : thus showing that she remembered her mother's excellent direction of being
satisfied with plain food. There was a
charming dessert, plenty of fruit; Serena ate
some, and enjoyed it: but she begged her
grandpapa would not give her wine ; she was
not accustomed to it at home, and therefore
preferred going without it. At first, grandpapa pressed her to take some; but when he

ound she really meant what she said, he praised her resolution, and forbore to tempt her any farther. After dinner, some company came in, and sat some time chatting; Serena continued silent the whole time they remained, amusing herself with looking at a book of pictures which she found on the window-seat.—"This is a quiet little girl," said one of the ladies. "She can be very merry, I assure you," answered her grandpapa. "Come here, Serena, and repeat one of your hymns to these ladies." Serena blushed; she felt afraid to repeat before strangers, she had not been used to it; but she knew she ought to obey her grandpapa. "Pray, my dear," continued her grandpapa, "repeat one of your little pieces—do, to oblige me." Serena's heart beat quick; but she approached her grandpapa's chair, and, leaning on the arm of it, asked him which hymn he would choose? "Any you please, my dear," said he. "I do not say them well, grandpapa, indeed I do not," said Serena, with a modest fear. "Do your best, then, my love," replied he. Serena recollected herself for a few minutes; then began to repeat Eve's Hymn. Her voice was low, and she trembled: but she was resolved to do her best; and, as she spoke distinctly, and did not hurry over her words, she got through pretty well. The ladies told her, considering she was so young, she had done very well; but that the obliging manner in which she had obeyed her grandfather, was better than the cleverest repeating in the world. They then went away. Serena was rejoiced that she had pleased them; but she thought in her own heart, that she did not love to speak before strangers. Once more alone with her grandpapa, she continued her gaiety, chatted, danced, and sang. When tired, she climbed on his knee, threw her arms round his neck, and, as her cheek rested on nis, told him how much she loved him, and how happy she was.

The tea came in, accompanied by some rich cake; Serena ate very sparingly of the latter, as she feared it might not agree with her. Her grandfather approved of her moderation.—"This cake is certainly not very proper for you; but the peas we had at dinner were very wholesome: why did you take so few?"—"I had enough, thank you grandpapa," said Serena.—"I suppose you thought," said her grandpapa, "that it was a very little dishful; but you know they are a great rarity at this early part of the summer."—"Yes, I know they are a rarity: they were the first I have seen," said Serena. "Do you not like them?"—"Indeed I do, grandpapa, very much."—"Ah! you cunning little girl! I see now the reason of your taking so few peas! You thought them a rarity; and, though you like them very much, you left

them for your poor old grandpapa?"—"Was
that wrong?"—"No, my dear child, it was
perfectly right; it was very considerate, and I
thank you; I am glad to find you are not a
greedy, selfish, girl." Here the conversation
was interrupted by the arrival of the servant,
who was come for Serena. "You shall stay
a little longer," said her grandpapa. "If you
please, let me go now," cried Serena; "mamma will expect me."—"You are tired of
being with me, then?'—"No, indeed, I am
not, grandpapa; I dearly love to be with
you: but I promised mamma I would return
soon, before it was dark."—"Go, then, my
dear Serena, and tell your mamma I am much
obliged to her for sending you to me; you
have been a very good girl." Serena tenderly
kissed her kind grandfather, and then, giving
her hand to the maid, she merrily tripped
homewards.

The weather was very fine; the sun, setting

behind the hills, tinged the purple clouds with a golden glow. The air was soft, and perfumed with wild flowers. Serena gathered a charming nosegay.—She recounted the pleasures of the past day, and her heart warmed with gratitude; she thought of the comforts of to-morrow, and her bosom glowed with hope. Happy child! blessed with health, with peace, with freedom, she knew and felt the blessings. She cast no discontented looks on richer or prouder mortals; she asked for no joys beyond her grasp. She came into this world to be happy, and by her virtues to make others so; she fulfilled her destiny, and the eye of Heaven beamed on her with benignity.

Serena met her parents a short distance from the house; they had strolled that way in expectation of seeing her.—" Ah! how glad I am that I did not stay!" thought Serena: "I should not then have met my dear father and mother; I should have disappointed them; I should have disappointed myself." She ran eagerly towards them; they each took a hand, and, thus happily placed, Serena doubly enjoyed the rest of her walk. She informed them of all she had seen or heard described; among other things, a new foot-cushion, which one of her cousins had worked and sent her grandpapa; it was done in worsteds, neatly shaded and finished. "How much I should like to do such a one for you, mamma!" said Serena.—"I suppose, my love, it is not difficult?"—"No, mamma, perfectly easy; and very pleasant work."—"If you think so, I will cheerfully get the materials for you."—"Thank you, mamma; I shall be so glad! And when I have a little time, I will begin it."—"A little time, Serena! What do you mean?"—"I mean, mamma, that at present so much seems on hand, that I had better wait for a day of leisure."—"By a day of leisure, if you mean a day without any occupation, Serena, I must say, I think you will wait in vain."—" Then, mamma, shall I never do it ? "—" I hope you will ; you have only to begin the work, and then it will always be ready for you to take up at every opportunity ; thus, by degrees, it will be completed, and no other business neglected."—" That is charming ! "— "It is thus, my dear Serena," said her father, " that many extensive works are perfected. Dr. Johnson, a writer, whom, I hope, you will one day read with equal pleasure and profit, remarks, 'that it is by small efforts, frequently repeated, that man completes his greatest undertakings, to have attempted which at one continued effort, would have baffled his ability.'—Fix this remark on your mind, it will be very useful to you in future life; and when once you have determined on the propriety or necessity of an undertaking, set about it with patient persever-

11*

ance, assured that in time it will repay your exertions. Perhaps this conversation is above your present comprehension, but it forcibly struck me as very apposite to your mother's opinion ; she will perhaps kindly simplify it for you."—" Will you, mamma ? " said Serena, with a look of entreaty. " Certainly, my dear," replied her mother ; " I will exemplify your father's observation, and that, I believe, is your favorite mode of illustration." —"Oh ! yes, mamma, I love your short stories."—" You remember the lace veil which I sent to your aunt ? "—" Yes, mamma, it was thought very elegant, and my aunt said it was a very handsome present."— " Well, my dear, that veil was a work of time. I was several years about it."—" I wonder you began it, mamma."—" Your aunt had done me great kindnesses ; I wished to make her some acknowledgment of my gratitude. I could not afford to buy her anything sufficiently valuable. I thought of netting a veil, which I knew would be both useful and handsome. This satisfied me on the propriety of so great an undertaking."—"And so you began it?"—"I did, with a secret resolution, however, that this employment should not interfere with any of my duties."—"What time did you find then to do it in?"—"I made it the companion of my few visits, both at home and abroad; and whilst the rest of the company played at cards, or sat unemployed, I produced my netting-case; and, though my progress was slow, yet it was certain. Sometimes, an hour occurred free from domestic duties; which also I gave to my netting. Thus, by seizing every opportunity, I at length completed my undertaking, and, last summer, had the inexpressible pleasure of presenting to your aunt this effort of my love and gratitude."—"How much it pleased her!"—"It did, my love; but my happiness was greater than hers."—"Mamma, I will begin the foot-stool."—"You shall, my dear; but it is necessary first to enquire whether what you are about to begin is worth finishing."—"Yes, it is, mamma, I am sure; for it will be useful to you, and look very neat besides."—"But, remember, whatever is begun must be properly completed; and no other business of the same nature undertaken till it is so."—"Ah! then I must finish my socks first."—"By all means; that is the occupation of your leisure now; when finished, I will readily prepare the materials of the foot-stool for you."—"You are very good, mamma!"—"Yes, Serena, let us not forget the old rule—one thing at a time." Thus ended Serena's happy visiting-day.

How many children, with equal means of pleasure, would have spent a day of vexation and disappointment! Serena produced in a great measure her own enjoyment. Her grandfather, though so kind, was an old man, and no playfellow; yet Serena, by endeavoring to amuse him, found herself amused. The dinner was good; Serena ate of it sparingly, and was refreshed. Had she been less moderate, and eaten a great deal, she would probably have been sick, and incapable of enjoying a merry afternoon. The ladies who called, distressed her for a moment, by asking her to repeat; but their praise of her obliging disposition more than made up for the momentary pain, and gave her a secret and lasting satisfaction. Had she been obstinate, or peevish, she would have been despised; and, whenever she remembered her behavior, her heart would have accused her. She faithfully fulfilled her mother's direction, and returned home immediately when the servant came for her. Had she neglected this direction, she would not only have missed the pleasure of meeting her parents, but probably incurred their displeasure, and thus closed her day with their deserved reproaches. Thus, then, never let us forget that it is in our power to turn everything to advantage; to make every incident bestow content, if not happiness: and that, when we complain of disappointment, we ought to look into our own breasts, and seek there for the cause; for there we shall most likely find it. Whilst we are peevish in our own bosoms, nothing that happens can please us; whilst we are contented in our bosoms, nothing that happens can make us entirely miserable. Serena always found it so; and so may every little girl, and every little boy, that heartily resolves to try it.

CHAPTER VIII.

Happiness to be found everywhere.—Town and Country
have both their own Advantages.—The Charms of early
Morning.—The Benefits of Activity.

THE next day, Serena accompanied her
mother in a walk to a farm at some distance:
as usual, she chatted as they went along.
" Mamma ! one of the ladies, yesterday, at
grandpapa's, patted me on the head, and said,
' Poor child, these are her best days; she will
never be so merry again.' What did that
mean, mamma ?   Does she think I shall be
miserable when I grow up ? "—" No, my
dear, not exactly that; but it is a common
idea with many grown-up people, that childhood is the happiest season of life."—" How
should that be, mamma ? "—" How should it
be indeed, Serena ! For my part I do not

understand it."—" Why, mamma, I should think, as I grow older, I shall know more, and so be happier!"—" True, my child, increase of knowledge must open new sources of happiness. Does not even the knowledge of reading give you many hours of amusement?" —" Yes, indeed, and writing too, mamma?" —" I could name many other acquirements that are sources of considerable enjoyment."— " Have you no pleasures, mamma?"—" Many, my child, very many. Yourself and your brother are sources of many of my sweetest joys; the society of your father—the power of pleasing him and you—these are *my* blessings."—" And old grandpapa, too, even he can be happy!"—" He can indeed, Serena; for he has to look back upon a blameless and useful life; he sees his children and grandchildren rising around him; he feels that he receives, and that he deserves, their respect and tenderness."—" Ah! mamma, I wish I

were older!"—"Stay, my child; every age
has its cares, as well as its enjoyments.
Your brother and yourself, in health, are
my joy; but in sickness, I think upon you
with an aching heart. Your father's society
is my dearest solace; but I cannot without many pangs behold the inroads of a
disorder that will too surely one day rob me
of this my best blessing. Your dear grandfather, feeble with age, feels every day his
strength departing from him, and finds himself
every hour less capable of enjoying the good
that surrounds him:—even you, Serena, you
have your cares."—"Ah! yes, mamma, when
I lost my brother's pretty rabbits; when I
make you, or papa, angry; when I neglect
my lesson, or am disappointed of any promised
pleasure."—"Thus, then, my dear little girl,
we have discovered, we have proved, that
every age has its good and evil: let us, then,
enjoy each period as it arrives—you are now

young and healthy."—" Yes! mamma, and
have many, oh! how many pleasures!"—
" Enjoy them, then, my sweet Serena, in
thankfulness to him who bestows them upon
you—and do not fear to grow old: increase
of age brings no increase of sorrow, whilst you
preserve your heart pure and blameless."—" I
hope, mamma, I shall be as happy when I am
old as dear grandpapa!"—" You must be as
good when you are young, then, as he was;
you must prepare for age as he did, by useful
and virtuous youth."—" I will, mamma, I
will; I will be happy always, for I will be
good always."

They had now reached the farm; and,
whilst her mother was inquiring about some
poultry, Serena diverted herself by observing
all that was going forward. In one corner, a
fine brood of young chickens were picking up
the grain, which their mother, the careful hen,
scratched up and showed them. The farmer's

daughter stood near watching their motions, for they were her chickens, and she daily fed them. "These are your chickens?" said Serena, addressing the little girl. "Yes ma'am, they are all my own, and I am so fond of them—and I have a lamb too; shall I show him to you?" Serena asked her mother's leave, and, having received it, followed the little girl to the home-field; there snug under the shelter of a hedge, lay a fat little lamb and its dam. They both jumped up, and came skipping to the call of their young mistress. Serena was delighted. "What a pretty creature!" she exclaimed; "how innocent it looks! how gentle!"—"It is very quiet, indeed," said the girl; "you shall see it feed from my hand." She then gathered a handful of fresh grass, which the lamb nibbled from her hand. In the same field, Serena saw a young calf, that was gamboling about in glee.—"Every thing

seems happy here," said Serena.—"Sure,
ma'am," answered her chubby-faced companion, " we have nothing to make us sad."
They returned through the garden ; it was
filled with various useful vegetables—the fra-
grant bean, the gay-flowered potato ; whilst
one little patch, alone devoted to flowers,
presented clusters of pinks, roses, and heart's-
ease. "This is my garden," said the little
girl; "father gave it to me, and I work here
every holiday." She gathered a charming
nosegay for Serena, who thankfully received
it. In leaving the garden, they passed a
clean pig-sty, where a large sow, and her litter
of twelve plump little pigs were all nestling
in their bed of straw. Serena thought she
never saw anything so comfortable. "What
else have I to show you?" said the little girl.
"Oh! the bee-hives."—"Will not the bees
sting you?" said Serena.—The girl laughed.
"No, sure, ma'am, unless indeed I were to

plague them, which I never do." The bee-hives were ranged under a sunny wall, over which a vine hung its rich festoons. The cottage casement peeped through the glossy leaves, whilst the hum of the busy bees soothed the listening ear. It was a scene of peaceful industry—it was a scene of rural beauty, of humble happiness. Serena, though young, felt all its charms, and stood gazing with unmixed delight. The voice of her mother calling for her, roused her; she thanked her attentive little guide, and has-tened to her mother, who had completed her commission, and they both took the way towards home. "Mamma," said Serena, after a few minutes' silence—" mamma, how comfortable every thing appeared at the farm !—how neat, how cheerful ! "—" Yes, my dear, I was much pleased with all I saw."—" And so was I, mamma. Oh ! how I wish I may always live in the country ! "—" The

12*

country has certainly many charms, Serena;
and there is a variety and gaiety in rural
occupations that is wonderfully pleasing."—
" And then, mamma, the beautiful landscapes,
the corn-fields, the rivers, the woods!"—" All
charming, Serena, all beautiful; all presenting
to us the finished, the perfect work of a
gracious God."—" Mamma, can a town have
any pleasures equal to these?"—" The pleasures of a town, Serena, are very different
from those of the country; yet, should you
ever reside in a town, it would be your duty
to find them out and to enjoy them."—" Well,
mamma, now I cannot find out a single pleasure—no walks, no views, nothing but close
streets and dusty lanes."—" You make me
smile, Serena, at your description. My dear
child, how many thousands of your fellow-
creatures fly to towns and cities, as the only
spots where enjoyment can be found!"—
" Mamma, is that possible?"—" Very pos-

sible, and very true, Serena."—"Then do tell me what they find so charming in a town."—"They find society, my dear,—a large, polished, and improving society!"— "That's true, mamma, to be sure; that I think must be very pleasant; but I fancy you cannot mention anything more."—"What think you, Serena, of enlarged means of instruction and improvement? Extensive libraries for the student—pictures for the painters: then, too, the various masters in every branch of art and science."—"Ah! these are advantages, indeed. mamma; how much I should like to possess them!"—"You must seek for them, then, where they can alone be found—in populous cities."—"Ah! I see there are particular advantages for every place and every station."—"There are, Serena; and it is a truth that can never be too frequently inculcated, for it leads to contentment with our lot, and a cheerful resignation

to our station in life, be it what it may."—
"Let me see, mamma; in the country, we
have pleasant walks, beautiful views, fresh air,
sweet flowers, and liberty to run and frisk
about whenever we please. In town, we
should have sensible acquaintance, delightful
libraries, pictures, and useful masters!"—
"Well summed up, Serena."—"Mamma, I
still love the country best!"—"I am glad of
it, my child; it is the scene where your
future life will most probably be laid—your
education has best fitted you for it: and let us
be thankful that our wishes and our fate are
thus happily united."

The conversation was here interrupted—
Serena saw her father at a distance; he had
an open letter in his hand, and seemed coming
to tell them some agreeable news. Serena
eagerly ran towards him, her mother also
quickened her pace: in a few minutes they
all met together.—"What news have you for

us, papa?" said Serena, half out of breath,
" A letter from Felix," said her father; " his
school will break up next Monday week, and
he longs to see us all!"—" And how we long
to see him!" cried Serena: " dear, dear
Felix!"—" I hope he is well," said his
mother. " Quite well," answered his father;
" but when Serena has recovered her breath,
she shall read this letter to you."—" Dear
papa," exclaimed Serena, " first tell me when
you will go for him?"

" Let me see," said her father; " his school
will break up on Monday, he says."—" Yes,
and you will go on Sunday, and be ready for
him," said the impatient Serena. " Gently,
my love," answered her father; " you know
I never travel on a Sunday."—" Only this
once, papa!"—" No, Serena: this is a matter of little importance, and ought not to
break into a long-established rule."—" But,
papa, many people travel on Sunday."—

"They do, my dear, and may perhaps be able to give good reasons for their conduct: I do not blame them; but, thinking as I do, their conduct cannot be an excuse for me. It shall not."—"But, papa, is there really any harm in travelling on a Sunday?"—"Serena! why was Sunday set apart from all the other days of the week?"—"For rest and devotion, papa!"—"Is either of these purposes answered by travelling? Tell me."—"Indeed it is not, papa."—"Then, my love, do we not oppose the express command of God, when we make Sunday a day of worldly business?"—"Dear papa! I did not think of that; I see now how wicked it is."—I am sure my little girl, that you now understand me, and will ever bear in mind that nothing but the most peremptory necessity should force us to occupy Sunday with business unworthy of its holy destination."—"Papa, I will endeavor always to remember this."—

"I think I must begin my journey on the Monday morning; and on Tuesday—"—" We shall once more embrace our dear Felix!"— " Restrain your raptures, Serena, or you will not have power to read this letter, which I know will give you great pleasure." Serena took the letter. " Shall I read it aloud?" said she.—" Do, my love," answered her mother. Serena thus began:

" My dear Father,

" How happy am I to tell you that our vacation will commence on Monday, 20th instant, and that I shall be ready any hour of that day to return with you to my dear home. What joy shall I have in again embracing my dear mother and sister! The latter I expect to find much grown and improved. Tell her, I hope she will think me improved also; for indeed, my dear father, I have very earnestly endeavored to attend to all my kind master's instructions. I like school very much; here are several very clever boys, and they are almost all very good-natured. The ushers, too, are very kind, and I never was happier in my life. Do not let Serena think from this, that I am sorry the holidays are approaching. Though I like school, I love home: here I can be very happy; but there I can never be miserable. Good-bye, dear papa; pray give my affectionate love and duty to mamma, and as many kisses as you please to Serena. I remain your ever dutiful and affectionate son,

FELIX.

"P. S. I suppose my garden is over-spread with weeds, and fancy I shall have a long job in clearing them away."

Serena smiled as she read this postscript. "He will be agreeably surprised," said she, "when he finds his garden without a single weed"—"He will, indeed," said her mother;

"and you, I think, will have almost as much pleasure in describing your industry in his service, as if you had to tell him, that, on his leaving us, you had cried yourself sick."—"I see, mamma, you are laughing at me," said Serena ; "and, indeed, I think I deserve it."

—"You would have deserved it, my love," replied her mother, "had you not heeded my advice; but as it is, you have two things to remember with pleasure."—"Two things, mamma! Which are they?"—"First, the satisfaction of having served your brother; and, secondly, that you did so in opposition to your own weaker feelings, and in obeying me."—"Mamma, you always tell me of some good, or of some pleasure."—"Happy should I be, my dear child, could my instructions, and my assistance, make your future life one scene of unbroken, unclouded peace ;—but we are at the end of our walk, and have now many pressing matters to arrange."

CHAPTER IX.

The Duty of Exertion.—Indolence a Crime.—How to
shorten a long Day.—Anxiety indulged leads to many
Mischiefs.

SERENA spent a happy week in anticipating
her brother's return. Every evening, she
watched the setting sun that closed another
day; she watched it with pleasure, for evening was welcome to her. Every morning, she
opened her eyes with new glee; the first
thought that rushed to her heart was, " I shall
soon see my brother!" She rose, she dressed herself, she wandered through the garden.
How charming are the fresh breezes of the
early morning! Serena felt them invigorate
her frame. "Felix will soon be here," she
exclaimed, as she wandered along; " he will
also say with me, how sweet are these

flowers! how green those fields!—We shall
again be together!—We shall be happy!—
Oh! how happy!"—Thus she indulged herself, until the hour of breakfast having arrived,
she entered the house with a face glowing
with health and joy.—"Mamma," she exclaimed, "I have had such a charming walk!
The garden is now so very pleasant! Everything so bright and beautiful!"—"I congratu-
late you, my love," answered her mother,
"on having tasted the charms of this fine
morning: it is one of our best country enjoyments."—"It is indeed, mamma; I wonder
how people can keep so much in bed, and
leave the sun to shine unadmired!"—"I
wonder so, too, Serena; and can only account for it by concluding, that, as they
never tried, they are ignorant of the peculiar
indulgence of early rising."—"But why do
they not try, mamma?"—"I suppose, my
love, they are too idle. Idleness, Serena, is

the great bane of human happiness. It palsies
the arm, it chills the heart, it deadens the
fancy. Were I called upon to name the
greatest enemy to felicity or to virtue, I
should without hesitation declare that enemy
to be idleness."—" I am sure of that, mamma ;
for if I had been idle, my brother's garden
would have been unweeded, his socks un-
finished, and, instead of being pleased, I
should have been discontented, cross, and
unhappy."—" You will find it so through
life, Serena ; and every day that you live will
prove to you that activity leads to numerous
enjoyments. You will recal my words, and
feel their truth."—" I feel that now, mamma :
for, though I am but a child, I know already
that there is greater pleasure in an early
morning's walk, than in all the sleeping and
dozing of the lazy sluggard."—" Yes, my
dear little girl ; and, as you grow older, I
hope you will also discover that a life of

active duty bestows joys beyond all that wealth and luxurious indolence has power to bestow. It bestows, Serena, peace of mind, —an approving conscience,—those greatest of earthly blessings."—"Exercise makes us healthy, too! Does it not, mamma?"—"It does, my love; it not only relieves many disorders, but prevents many. Indeed, I know more than one instance, in which air and exercise alone perfectly re-established a very crazy and shattered constitution." —"How was that, dear mamma! Do tell me."—"A lady, my love, who, having weak spirits, thought, therefore, she had weak health, and fancied herself unequal to any exertion. She lay till late in bed, walked little in the air, took medicine, and so enfeebled herself by this management, that she was at last what she had feared to be, a helpless invalid."—"Poor creature! How sad!"—"Yes, Serena, very sad indeed; for

13*

she was a wife and a mother."—" Her poor
children, mamma !"—" And her poor husband, my dear, both were to be pitied."—
" And did she die soon ? "—" She would,
most assuredly. had not a true friend discovered to her her real state, and that nothing
but exertion could possibly save her life."—
" And what did she do, mamma ? "—" She
made a good resolution, and very wisely kept
it—she altered all her plans—she rose early,
she took long walks, she superintended her
garden, assisted in the education of her children, and overlooked the business of her
house."—" And what became of her, mamma ? "—" She is at this moment the healthiest
and happiest woman of my acquaintance.
With her fears vanished her low spirits, she
gained cheerfulness as well as strength, and
lives to be the comfort and support of her
family and friends."—" That was a happy
end to her story, mamma ! "—" It was. my

dear, and would be so to that of many others. But we must now attend to our own duties."

The long-wished-for Monday at length arrived. Serena saw her father depart, without a sigh. He was going for her brother; that dear friend and companion, whose society she had so long missed, whose presence she was so soon again to enjoy. "This day will seem very long to me, mamma," said Serena. "You have spoken very accurately, my dear; it will *seem*, it will not really *be* longer," replied her mother, smilingly. "That is true, mamma; but if I think so, I shall feel it so, you know."—"You are quite a logician, Serena: however, as the matter depends on your own feelings, the only remedy must be to change them."—"Change my feelings, mamma!"—"You are anxious, uneasy, unfit for any business—restless."—"Mamma, you are a conjuror! You have so exactly described what I feel."—"Well, then, I will

continue my conjuration, and put this unavail-
ing anxiety to flight."—" Ah! mamma, if
you could do that, you would be a conjuror
indeed."—" Where is your work-basket?"—
" I cannot work, mamma."—" Nay, Serena,
if you will not make the slightest exertion to
forward my plan, I certainly cannot relieve
you."—" But work is so tiresome now, when
my heart is full of other matters."—" Physic
is unpleasant, Serena, and yet often gives ease
from pain."—" Mamma, here is my work-
basket." Serena said this with a melancholy
air; she sighed often, and looked thoughtful.
Her mother, by degrees, drew her to take
interest in her work. Serena's brow became
less clouded. When the work was completed,
her mother desired her to read her a little
story; she did so, and was much amused.
They walked in the garden, and when the
clock sounded the hour for dinner, Serena
started " Bless me! Is it so late?" said

she. After dinner the flower-pots were filled with fresh-gathered roses. This was a delightful employment; Serena exerted all her taste in the disposal of her flowers, and when she replaced them on the stands, her mother highly admired her judicious arrangement. The rabbits were next visited and fed; some fruit was gathered; and, as Serena and her mother sat under a shady tree, eating it, they had a great deal of entertaining conversation. As a great indulgence, Serena's attentive mother ordered the tea-table to be brought out, and permitted Serena to perform the honors of it. "How much I enjoy my tea in this bower!" exclaimed Serena. "Yes, my love," answered her mother, "the balmy air wafting around us, the open view of the surrounding country, the warbling of birds and the fragrance of flowers, give great zest to our feelings, and invigorate and enliven our thoughts. A room, however airy, cannot

bestow these enjoyments, thus pure, thus un-
bounded."—" Indeed, mamma, it cannot ;—
the pleasure of helping you, how I enjoy it
too !" The sun was now beginning to lose
the splendor of its glory, and was sinking in
milder beauty over the distant hills. Serena
and her mother left their bower, and sauntered
through the surrounding fields and woods.
They mounted the heath, they skirted the
river. Nature, ever charming, ever new,
offered them variety of beauty. The village
bell chimed eight as Serena drew towards her
home. "Mamma, is it possible? Can it be
so ?"—she exclaimed. "Is it indeed so
late ?"—"It is, indeed, my love,"—"How
swiftly then, this day has passed!"—"Yet I
thought you expected a long day. Can you
account for this, Serena ?"—"Oh! yes, that
I can, mamma! I have been employed ; I
have been amused ; I have not thought of the
time."—"In future, then, you will know how

Felix and Serena in the Garden.

to make an expected long day seem a short day, Serena."—" Yes, mamma ; and for this knowledge, as for every other. I must thank you!" The grateful child threw her little arms round her mother's neck ; she kissed her cheek ; she felt the pleasure of gratitude, the joy of expressing it. " My Serena !" said her mother, as she tenderly returned her caresses—" my Serena ! if you feel such . gratitude to me for opening your heart to joy how thankful ought you to be to the gracious God who gave you a heart capable of feeling it ! If I have obliged you, by pointing out to you the sources of happiness, how boundless is your obligation to that great God, who *created* these sources of happiness ! To Him, then, let your soul arise in never-ceasing praise ! From Him springs all your felicity in this world—on Him rest all your hopes of the world to come. My dearest child ! never forget the sacred ties that bind you to your

God and Father in Heaven." The heart of Serena was deeply affected; her little bosom glowed with devotion. Her mother observed with transport the sacred impression. They finished their walk in silence; but the moment they entered the house Serena flew to her chamber, and, throwing herself on her knees, breathed out her evening sacrifice of prayer and praise.

It was Tuesday—"This evening my brother will be here," thought Serena, as she first opened her eyes to the day. She remembered her yesterday's recipe for shortening a long day. She applied herself with assiduity to her lessons; she worked; she read. Dinner-hour arrived: the afternoon was passed in a variety of lighter occupations; at length, the evening began to close. With a palpitating heart Serena listened to every sound, and more than once the gardener's wheelbarrow brought her breathless to the window. She rejoiced when she saw this teasing wheel-barrow and the gardener retire for the night. All now was still, save the distant whistle of the returning laborer, or the short barkings of his attendant dog. Serena, anxious and agitated, sat silently watching the slow hand of the revolving clock. It pointed at nine. Serena sighed heavily.—"Mamma, I fear they will not come to-night!" said she. "I begin to fear so too, my love." Serena's eyes filled with tears. "Then, mamma, I dare say, some accident has happened."—"No, my child, I trust not ; the weather has been fine, the roads are excellent :—I cannot think any accident has happened."—"Then Felix is taken ill, or, perhaps, papa."———"Let us not torture ourselves with these cruel fears, Serena ; we have no present means of ascertaining the truth, and, if all prove safe, we shall be uselessly embittering these hours."—'But if all be not safe mamma ?"—"Then

14

still, my dear, we are wrong to be thus wearing out our strength and spirits; it will render us incapable of giving assistance, should our worst fears be true."—" Mamma! how can you account for their not being here?"— "Many circumstances, my dear, may have arisen to detain them."—" But then papa would have written."—" He might have been prevented; or perhaps he has written, and the letter has miscarried, or will arrive to-morrow. When we are in the power of so many events, my dear Serena, let us not fear the worst, but rather hope the best. Hope was given us to soothe the hours of despondency, and never can we better call in its aid than in such a moment as this."—" And do not you fear too, mamma?"—" I will not pretend to say, Serena, that I am as happy as if our dear travellers had punctually arrived."—" Oh! no, mamma! that is impossible."—" It is impossible, Serena; yet at the same time, I think it my duty to make my reason so far master my feelings, that they shall not lead me to ungrateful murmurings, or impious regrets."—" Dear mother, your eyes even now are full of tears."—"Do not, then, increase my weakness, Serena, by your fears; we must comfort each other, and not harass each other."—Serena felt the full force of this observation ; she saw how much her mother struggled for composure, and resolved to imitate her fortitude. She wiped away her tears, she checked her sobs, she silenced her gloomy anticipation, she even spoke cheerfully to her mother. Ten o'clock arrived. Serena's mother became pale and exhausted ; the affectionate little girl forgot her own disappointment ; she hastened to her mother, she soothed her with endearments, she enlivened her with hope. The servant entered with refreshments. To oblige Serena, her mother ate some chicken and drank a

little wine : Serena did so too.   " Thank you,
my child," said her mother, affectionately
embracing her, " you have been a great comfort to me this evening." Serena felt herself
repaid for all her exertions.—" We will now
go to bed," continued her mother, "and try
to sleep, that we may gain strength for the
duties of to-morrow, whatever they may be."
Serena obeyed in silence ; and after fervently
praying for the safety of the two dear travellers, they both retired to their pillows.

CHAPTER X.

False Sensibility.—The Blessings of Home.—Conclusion

ANOTHER day was passed in painful suspense —no letter—no tidings of the travellers. Serena was miserable; it was in vain that she admired her mother's patient resignation; it was in vain that she endeavored to imitate it: her feelings were not sufficiently under her control; they overwhelmed her reason. "My dear Serena," said her mother, in a mild tone, "I hope, as you grow older, you will gain the ascendancy of your feelings, or they will otherwise be the source of many sorrows to you. Such trials as these are common in life, and we ought to be prepared for them Should the event be as you fear, will these tears prepare you for supporting distress with

14*

fortitude? Should it be otherwise, should all prove safe and well, with what self-reproach will you look back on so many hours lost in causeless regrets!" Serena promised patience.—"Come, then, my love, let us go to our supper; we made a bad dinner, and must now try to behave better." Serena sat down to the table, but she could not eat; her mother, however, took something.—"Mamma, how can you eat? I am sure I cannot— there is such a choking in my throat," said Serena. "That is a nervous affection, Serena, produced by indulged anxiety. At your age, it may be conquered; hereafter you may try in vain."—"Indeed, mamma, I cannot help it."—"Indeed, my love, you can. Make the attempt; I will ensure success." Serena took one mouthful, it was unpleasant to her; she, however, persisted, and soon felt the choking in her throat removed.—"Mamma, this is surprising; I am better already."—"You see

how much we can do towards curing ourselves. I have known many little girls who
indulged themselves by allowing every little
distress to overcome them, till they became so
weak, that their tears would continually be
flowing, and they became complete hysteric
ladies."—" What are hysterics, mamma?"—
" A violent burst of tears, my dear, indulged
without restraint on trivial occasions; so I
define it."—" But can we stop our tears,
mamma?"—" Certainly, my love; the thinking that they cannot be stopped is, however,
the cause why so many are shed by a weak
and idle *sensibility*."—" Mamma, you said
that ironically."—" Sensibility, Serena, is a
word that is so generally misused, that I
must confess it never passes my lips without
raising ridiculous ideas; for I have heard the
most direct selfishness called an exquisite
sensibility."—" How could that possibly be,
mamma?"—" In scenes of distress, Serena,

when I see a young lady, regardless of the
immediate object of commiseration, throwing
herself into an agony of useless tears,—when
I see those attentions that are due to the real
sufferer, claimed by the exquisitely sensitive
observer,—I turn with disgust from such an
affected and selfish display of unfelt sympathy."—"Ah! yes, mamma, I remember
what you said in the cottage—that to relieve
is better than to pity."—"I am glad you
have so well remembered, my dear. It was
on the same principle that just now I wished
you to eat something, and not continue to
exhaust yourself."—"Was it, mamma?"—
"Yes, my dear; for though I know that to
eat is against every rule of *exquisite sensibility*.
yet I also know that, without some support,
the human frame must sink into uselessness.
In attending the sick-bed of a beloved friend
or relation, it is an essential part of our duty
to take some care of ourselves. If we do not.

what is the consequence?—The invalid, just recovered from sickness, has the painful conviction that his nurse has suffered by her cares for him, and very probably has in his turn to watch over her pillow, and support her who ought to have supported herself."

The sound of a distant carriage now drew Serena's attention—she flew to the door: it drew nearer—she scarcely breathed—another moment, and a chaise drove up to the door. What a joyous moment for Serena!—she beheld her father and brother—she was locked in their embrace—she heard their well-known voices.—" Both safe, both well !" exclaimed the transported Serena.—" Ah! how happy I am ! "—" You need not say so, my child," replied her mother; " your eyes are sufficiently expressive."—" And are you, indeed, so happy ?" said her father, archly looking at her. " Can you doubt it, papa? I am sure he cannot," said Serena. " You feel, then,

the pang of parting somewhat repaid!"—
"Oh! yes, repaid—more than repaid—I
never felt such joy before."—"Did I not tell
you, Serena, that we must purchase our dearest joy by some previous trials?"—"It is so,
indeed. papa. But we expected you on
Monday."—Did you not receive my father's
letter?" said Felix. "No, my love."—"I
fear, then, you have been very anxious about
us," continued Felix. "We will not talk of
that now," said his mother: "observe only,
my Serena, how wrong we should have
been to allow our fears seriously to oppress
us."—"But there seemed to be cause, mamma."—"Let us, then, from this instance,
learn to act only from what *is*, not what
seems. Thus shall we save ourselves many
hours of causeless sorrow. We will now,
however, speak only of joy and of gratitude "
—"How much Serena is improved!" said
Felix; "and, dear mother, how well you

iook! Ah! certainly, there is nothing in this world so dear, so very dear, as home."— "May you always think so, my boy! And may you always possess a peaceful and an endeared home! But, come, we are very hungry; pray give us something to eat." The supper-table was soon replenished with fresh viands. The happy family surrounded it with joyous faces. Serena often rose from her seat to press the hand of Felix, and whisper to him the overflowings of her heart.

The next day brought with it new enjoyments. Serena, hanging on the arm of her brother, led the way to his garden. "I suppose it is covered with weeds," said he. Serena only smiled, and they proceeded. Arrived at the spot, what was the surprise of Felix, to behold the expected scene of desolation blooming with flowers, the weeds destroyed, the shrubs pruned—all neat, all owning the hand of careful cultivation!

15

" Dear Serena ! " he tenderly exclaimed, " this is your doing—your industry has been exerted here."—" Yes, brother, it was my work ; but you are indebted for it to mamma."—" How is that, Serena ? "—" I can soon tell you. When you left us at Easter. I, like a silly simpleton, sat crying in a corner, miserable myself, and useless to others."— " And mamma roused you ! "—" She did, and showed me how foolish my behavior was ; and now, Felix, I feel how right she was ; for my industry has pleased you, and I am happy."—" Thank you, my dear girl," cried Felix ; " you thought of me when I was far away, and worked for me when I could not work for myself."—" And now, brother, I am so glad I have done something that would please you ; for in one matter I fear you will be angry."—" Angry with my little attentive gardener ! That is impossible ! "—Serena then, with many blushes, informed her brother of the sad story of the young rabbits. When she had finished it, "Will you forgive me, Felix," added she, "for my neglect? I suffered so much, that I am sure I shall never put off a duty again." Felix affectionately kissed her, and assured her of his entire forgiveness. "And besides," added he, "if this circumstance has cured you of a fault, I shall be almost glad that it happened. So, good, you see, Serena, may be drawn even from evil."

Thus happily passed this day, and every day of the life of Felix and Serena. By the advice of their kind parents, supported by their own unceasing exertions, they conquered their faults ; and, by doing so, prepared themselves to enjoy the many blessings that surrounded them. In sickness they were patient ; in sorrow they were resigned. They knew that riches could not confer happiness, and therefore did not covet them ; they knew that

titles could not confer peace, and therefore did
not ask for them. They discovered that in
our own hearts lies the secret of happiness.
There, then, they searched for felicity—there
they found it. Yet troubles often assailed
them; but whilst their consciences whispered
peace, they smiled at the little evils of life,
and bowed with humility to its greater sorrows.
Were they sick, they looked forward to the
hour of health, and bore uncomplainingly the
inevitable lot of humanity. But in the days
of health and prosperity, they remembered
the gracious God who thus blessed them, and
so remembering, doubled every blessing they
enjoyed.

Felix, without any remarkable share of
ability, engaged assiduously in the profession
which his father selected for him. By a
course of steady and persevering exertion, he
gained an honorable station in life. He was
honest, he was charitable, he was pious. His

sacred regard to truth remained with him through life, and ensured to him the respect of all who knew him; whilst the cheerfulness of his manners, and the benevolence of his heart, rendered him beloved by all. Thus. by gradual improvement, the petulant boy became a worthy and respectable man. The helpless child grew into an useful member of society.

Serena, too,—the little, careless, idle Serena! Behold her, the amiable daughter, the affectionate sister—the faithful friend. A few years of attentive care has made this wondrous change; has transformed the thoughtless girl into the sensible woman See her cheering the latter days of her excellent parents, repaying them, by a thousand attentions, their care of her infancy, their instruction of her childhood. She learned music, but she did not learn it to forget it. She makes a more valuable use of this acquirement, for she

15*

exerts it to cheer her parents. When the evening is dark, when the rain beats on the window, and the wind howls through the leafless trees, Serena gaily flies to her piano-forte; ner fingers run lightly over the keys; her voice, feeble, yet cheering, accompanies the notes. Now she warbles the sportive tones of glee and merriment, and now swells to sacred melody of prayer and praise! Who directs the household cares,—provides the neat, though frugal meal,—regulates the duties of the day, and smiles away its cares? —The active, the useful Serena. Who bends over the sick couch of an aged father, and speaks comfort to an anxious mother's heart? —The gentle Serena.

And is all this possible?—My youthful readers, be assured it is: be assured, that you can every one of you prove a Felix or a Serena; that, whatever be your faults, you can, by God's help, conquer them; what-

ever your virtues, you may improve them:
--make, then, the experiment. For your
cwn sakes—for the sake of all that are dear
to you—make the experiment. It cannot
fail of success. The very endeavor will
bestow joy. For, bear in your minds, and
never let it escape from your memories—
that you need only be Always Good, and
then you will assuredly be ALWAYS HAPPY.

NEW AND ATTRACTIVE JUVENILES,

Just Published.

TRAVELS AND SURPRISING ADVENTURES OF
BARON MUNCHAUSEN,

Illustrated with 11 full-page, and 22 smaller Engravings. 75 cts.

THE LIFE AND ADVENTURES OF ROBINSON CRUSOE.

By DANIEL DE FOE, including a Memoir of the Author, with an Essay on his writings. Printed on tinted paper, and beautifully illustrated by THWAITES. 63 cts.

PEBBLES FROM JORDAN;
OR,
BIBLE EXAMPLES OF EVERY-DAY TRUTH.

By MISS GRAHAM, with Engravings by J. A. ADAMS. 38 cts.

BLIND ARTHUR, AND OTHER STORIES:

Being a collection of "Moral Lessons and Stories on the Proverbs," designed to render some of those inspired sayings more easy and familiar to children. By JANE STRICKLAND. Illustrated by J. A. ADAMS. 38 cts.

LILIES FROM LEBANON;
OR,
SCRIPTURE SKETCHES.

By MISS GRAHAM, embellished with 8 beautiful Wood-cuts by ADAMS. 38 cts.

THE CHILD'S OWN
PICTURE AND VERSE BOOK.

Selected and arranged from the best authorities, by a "Grandfather." Illustrated with 100 full-page Engraving. Plain. 75 cts.; colored, $1.00.

FAVORITE FAIRY TALES
FOR LITTLE FOLKS.

With 70 Illustrations by THWAITES and others, engraved by the best artists. 75 cts.

AMY DEANE,

And other Tales.

BY VIRGINIA F. TOWNSEND.

ILLUSTRATED.

NEW YORK:
PUBLISHED BY JAMES MILLER,
(SUCCESSOR TO C. S. FRANCIS & CO..)
522 BROADWAY.

NEW AND BEAUTIFUL JUVENILES,

PUBLISHED BY

JAMES MILLER,

No. 522 BROADWAY.

THE CHILD'S OWN PICTURE AND VERSE BOOK. Selected and arranged from the best authorities. By a "Grandfather." Illustrated with 100 full page engravings. 75c.

The Same, elegantly colored. $1.00.

FAVORITE FAIRY TALES FOR LITTLE FOLKS, with 70 engravings, by Thwaites and others. Cloth, 50c.

ILLUMINATED HOUSEHOLD STORIES FOR LITTLE FOLKS, being a collection of popular Fairy Tales. Beautifully illustrated. $1.00.

FAIRY LIBRARY FOR LITTLE FOLKS, containing the following, now ready—

RED RIDING HOOD,	PUSS IN BOOTS,
CINDERELLA,	GOODY TWO-SHOES,
JACK THE GIANT-KILLER,	BEAUTY AND THE BEAST,
BLUE BEARD,	JACK AND THE BEAN
TOM THUMB,	STALK,

ALADDIN, OR THE WONDERFUL LAMP.

In paper covers, 12c. each.

The Same, large edition, with frontispiece printed in oil colors 25c. each.

ROBINSON CRUSOE. A new and beautiful edition. Profusely illustrated from drawings by Thwaites. 50c.

MOTHER GOOSE'S MELODIES. A new edition, with illustrations by American artists. 25c.

THE MAGIC RING,

AND OTHER

ORIENTAL FAIRY TALES.

FROM THE GERMAN OF HERDER, LIEBESKIND, AND KRUMMACHER.

ILLUSTRATED.

EL RAKHAM.

NEW YORK:

JAMES MILLER, 522 BROADWAY.

JAMES MILLER,

Bookseller, Publisher, and Importer,

522 BROADWAY, NEW YORK,

OPPOSITE THE ST. NICHOLAS HOTEL,

Has for sale a very complete and extensive stock of

ENGLISH AND AMERICAN BOOKS,

IN THE VARIOUS DEPARTMENTS OF LITERATURE;

INCLUDING

STANDARD EDITIONS OF THE BEST AUTHORS IN

HISTORY, BIOGRAPHY, BELLES-LETTRES, ETC.

FINELY BOUND IN MOROCCO, CALF, ETC., FOR

DRAWING-ROOM LIBRARIES;

LIKEWISE ORNAMENTED AND RICHLY EMBELLISHED BOOKS
OF PLATES FOR THE CENTRE-TABLE.

*** Particular attention given to orders from Public and Private Libraries.

ENGLISH AND AMERICAN PERIODICALS

supplied and served carefully and faithfully to Subscribers throughout the city, or sent by mail to the country. Orders from any part of the world, with a remittance or reference for payment in New York, will be promptly attended to.

IMPORTATION OF ALL BOOKS & PERIODICALS

for which he may receive orders, a small commission only being charged for the business. The same attention given to an order for a single copy as for a quantity.

BOOK BINDING IN ALL ITS BRANCHES.

"If this lady is not a great Poet, who is!"—Frazer's Mag.

ELIZABETH BARRETT BROWNING'S

P O E M S,

4 Vols., Blue and Gold, $3.00.

AURORA LEIGH,

AND OTHER POEMS;

Blue and Gold, 75 Cents.

LAST POEMS;

Blue and Gold, 75 Cents.

"Mrs. Browning's Poems are marked by strength of passion, by intensity of emotion, and by high religious aims, sustained and carried out by an extraordinary vigor of imagination and felicity of expression. * * * It is pleasant to find a writer of such unquestioned ability as Mrs. Browning, and with a love of nature so pure and healthy, turning away from the pantheistic tendencies of the age, and from the exclusive love and worship of nature, to recognize, in simplicity of soul, the graces and sanctities of a Christian faith, and to dwell amid the beloved and hallowed scenes which a Christian heart and imagination can create around us."—*Christian Register.*

THE

DREAM OF LITTLE TUK,

And other Tales.

BY HANS CHRISTIAN ANDERSEN.

New York:
Published by James Miller,
(SUCCESSOR TO C. S. FRANCIS & CO.)
522 Broadway.

THE CHILD'S OWN
TREASURY
OF
FAIRY TALES.

Illustrated by 120 Engravings,

AFTER DESIGNS BY EMINENT AMERICAN ARTISTS.

NEW YORK:

JAMES MILLER, 522 BROADWAY.

NEW AND ATTRACTIVE JUVENILES,
Just Published.

TRAVELS AND SURPRISING ADVENTURES OF
BARON MUNCHAUSEN.

Illustrated with 11 full-page, and 22 smaller Engravings. **75 cts.**

THE LIFE AND ADVENTURES OF ROBINSON CRUSOE.

By DANIEL DE FOE, including a Memoir of the Author, with an Essay on his writings. Printed on tinted paper, and beautifully illustrated by THWAITES. **63 cts.**

PEBBLES FROM JORDAN;
OR,
BIBLE EXAMPLES OF EVERY-DAY TRUTH.

By MISS GRAHAM, with Engravings by J. A. ADAMS. **38 cts.**

BLIND ARTHUR, AND OTHER STORIES:

Being a collection of "Moral Lessons and Stories on the Proverbs," designed to render some of those inspired sayings more easy and familiar to children. By JANE STRICKLAND. Illustrated by J. A. ADAMS. **38 cts.**

LILIES FROM LEBANON;
OR,
SCRIPTURE SKETCHES.

By MISS GRAHAM, embellished with 8 beautiful Wood-cuts by ADAMS. **38 cts.**

THE CHILD'S OWN
PICTURE AND VERSE BOOK.

Selected and arranged from the best authorities, by a "Grandfather." Illustrated with 100 full-page Engraving. Plain, **75 cts.**; colored, **$1.00.**

FAVORITE FAIRY TALES
FOR LITTLE FOLKS.

With 70 Illustrations by THWAITES and others, engraved by the best artists. **75 cts.**

POPULAR
AIRY TALES
for Little Folks.

WITH SIXTY ILLUSTRATIONS BY THWAITES AND OTHERS,

ENGRAVED BY THE BEST ARTISTS.

NEW YORK:
JAMES MILLER, 522 BROADWAY.

The Travels

AND

SURPRISING ADVENTURES

OF

BARON MUNCHAUSEN.

ILLUSTRATED BY ALFRED CROWQUILL.

NEW YORK:

JAMES MILLER, 522 BROADWAY.

THE

BOYS' BOOK

OF INDIAN

Battles and Adventures,

WITH ANECDOTES ABOUT THEM.

ILLUSTRATED WITH TEN ENGRAVINGS

BY THE AUTHOR OF "EVENINGS IN BOSTON," "RAMON
THE ROVER OF CUBA," ETC.

New York:
JAMES MILLER, 522 BROADWAY.

THE STORY

OF

CECIL AND HIS DOG.

Illustrated.

JAMES MILLER, NEW YORK.

AMY DEANE,

And other Tales.

BY VIRGINIA F. TOWNSEND.

ILLUSTRATED.

NEW YORK:
PUBLISHED BY JAMES MILLER,
(SUCCESSOR TO C. S. FRANCIS & CO.,)
522 BROADWAY.

MOTHER GOOSE'S MELODIES.

CONTAINING

ALL THAT HAVE EVER COME TO LIGHT

OF

Her Memorable Writings.

ILLUSTRATED THROUGHOUT WITH ENGRAVINGS FROM ORIGINAL
DESIGNS BY AMERICAN ARTISTS.

NEW YORK:
JAMES MILLER, 522 BROADWAY.

ALWAYS HAPPY;

OR

Anecdotes

OF

FELIX AND HIS SISTER SERENA.

NEW YORK:

PUBLISHED BY JAMES MILLER,

(SUCCESSOR TO C. S. FRANCIS & CO.,)

522 BROADWAY.

MDCCCLXIII.

THE CHILD'S OWN
TREASURY OF FAIRY TALES.

Embracing the best and most popular of the old
fashioned Fairy Tales, and Illustrated
in the highest style of Art.

———

FAVORITE FAIRY TALES
FOR LITTLE FOLKS.

With 70 Illustrations by THWAITES and others.

———

POPULAR FAIRY TALES
FOR LITTLE FOLKS.

With 60 Illustrations from original designs.

———

This series of Fairy Stories has for generations
been listened to and read by children with a delight which all others have failed to afford them.

That these editions may be more perfect than
any others extant, they have been embellished with
exquisite specimens of high Pictorial Art, from
which children may derive those correct ideas that
will mature into the beautiful and grand.

THE FAVORITE SCHOLAR,

BY MARY HOWITT.

AND OTHER TALES,

BY MRS. S. C. HALL, CHARLES COWDEN CLARK, AND JAMES
D. HAAS.

NEW YORK:
PUBLISHED BY JAMES MILLER
(SUCCESSOR TO C. S. FRANCIS & CO.,)
522 BROADWAY

NEW AND BEAUTIFUL JUVENILES,

PUBLISHED BY

JAMES MILLER,

No. 522 BROADWAY.

THE CHILD'S OWN PICTURE AND VERSE BOOK. Selected and arranged from the best authorities. By a "Grandfather." Illustrated with 100 full page engravings. 75c.

The Same, elegantly colored. $1.00.

FAVORITE FAIRY TALES FOR LITTLE FOLKS, with 70 engravings, by Thwaites and others. Cloth, 50c.

ILLUMINATED HOUSEHOLD STORIES FOR LITTLE FOLKS, being a collection of popular Fairy Tales. Beautifully illustrated. $1.00.

FAIRY LIBRARY FOR LITTLE FOLKS, containing the following, now ready—

RED RIDING HOOD,	PUSS IN BOOTS,
CINDERELLA,	GOODY TWO-SHOES,
JACK THE GIANT-KILLER,	BEAUTY AND THE BEAST,
BLUE BEARD,	JACK AND THE BEAN
TOM THUMB,	STALK,

ALADDIN, OR THE WONDERFUL LAMP.

In paper covers, 12c. each.

The Same, large edition, with frontispiece printed in oil colors, 25c. each.

ROBINSON CRUSOE. A new and beautiful edition. Profusely illustrated from drawings by Thwaites. 50c.

MOTHER GOOSE'S MELODIES. A new edition, with illustrations by American artists. 25c.

THE MAGIC RING,

AND OTHER

ORIENTAL FAIRY TALES.

FROM THE GERMAN OF HERDER, LIEBESKIND, AND KRUMMACHER.

ILLUSTRATED.

EL RAKHAM.

NEW YORK:

JAMES MILLER, 522 BROADWAY.

AMY DEANE,

AND OTHER STORIES.

BY VIRGINIA F. TOWNSEND.

Beautifully Illustrated.

The interesting character of these stories, and the high moral tone which, without becoming tedious, pervades them all, recommends this book in a special manner to our Young Friends. The Publisher is satisfied that on perusal it will be found to compare favorably with any of the tales of Mary Howitt, Miss Edgeworth, Mrs. Hofland, &c., &c.

THE MAGIC RING,

AND OTHER ORIENTAL FAIRY TALES.

ILLUSTRATED.

The same simplicity of style and elegance of language, which have rendered the "Arabian Nights" so justly popular, will be found in the above book, which the Publisher now offers, and which will, he is confident, when better known, take rank amongst our most Popular Juvenile Literature.

THE FAVORITE SCHOLAR.

By MARY HOWITT,

AND OTHER TALES.

NEW AND ATTRACTIVE

JUVENILES

JUST PUBLISHED BY JAMES MILLER.

THE DREAM OF LITTLE TUK,

AND OTHER TALES.

BY HANS CHRISTIAN ANDERSEN.

Illustrated. 50 cts.

THE STORY OF CECIL AND HIS DOG

Illustrated. 75 cts.

Claudine, and the Garland of Everlastings.

Illustrated. 63 cts.

RIGHT AND WRONG, & THE GOLD CROSS.

Illustrated. 63 cts.

ALWAYS HAPPY;

Or, Anecdotes of Felix and his Sister Serena.

Illustrated. 63 cts.

The Well in the Rock, and Other Stories.

BY VIRGINIA F. TOWNSEND.

Illustrated. 75 cts.

NEW AND ATTRACTIVE

JUVENILES,

Just Published.

AMY DEANE,

AND OTHER STORIES.

By VIRGINIA F. TOWNSEND.

Illustrated. 75 cts.

THE CHILD'S OWN

TREASURY OF FAIRY TALES.

Containing the best and most popular Fairy Tales.

Beautifully Illustrated. Square 16mo. $1.

THE MAGIC RING,

AND OTHER ORIENTAL TALES.

Illustrated. 75 cts.

THE CHILD'S

HOME STORY BOOK.

A Collection of unexceptionable Tales by MISS STRICKLAND and MISS GRAHAM. Illustrated by 24 beautiful Engravings.
Square 16mo. 75 cts.

THE BOY'S BOOK OF

INDIAN BATTLES & ADVENTURES.

WITH ANECDOTES ABOUT THEM.

10 Engravings. 75 cts.

FAVORITE
FAIRY TALES
FOR LITTLE FOLKS.

With Seventy Illustrations by Thwaites and others,

ENGRAVED BY THE BEST ARTISTS.

NEW YORK:

JAMES MILLER, 522 BROADWAY.

Published by James Miller, 522 Broadway.

THE FAVORITE SCHOLAR,

By Mary Howitt.

And Other Tales. 63 cts.

THE BOY'S BOOK OF

INDIAN BATTLES & ADVENTURES,

WITH ANECDOTES ABOUT THEM. 75 cts.

TRAVELS AND SURPRISING ADVENTURES OF

BARON MUNCHAUSEN.

Illustrated with 10 full-page, and 22 smaller Engravings. 75 cts.

A M Y   D E A N E,

AND OTHER STORIES.

BY VIRGINIA F. TOWNSEND.

75 cts.

THE CHILD'S OWN

TREASURY OF FAIRY TALES.

Containing the best and most popular Fairy Tales.

Beautifully Illustrated. Square 16mo. $1.

www.ingramcontent.com/pod-product-compliance
Lightning Source LLC
Chambersburg PA
CBHW031955060726
47497CB00016B/2223